The Fate of Us

Rachel Bowdler

Part I

Whitby, 2017: The First Hello

One

The pocket watch cannot be fixed. No matter how often he taps the face or adjusts the cogs, the minute hand remains frozen on the VI and the hour half past the X — though he'd been sure he heard it ticking when he'd first picked it up from the soil.

Ten thirty. Such an arbitrary time, even for this grotty, rusted, sad little thing. He clicks it closed and slides it into the front pocket of his shirt as defeat sets in.

His disappointment is forgotten when he looks up a second later.

The sight of her grooming the horses brings a peace he has never known before — one that he cannot explain and would not dare try to. He knows, though, that if he ever found a home, it would feel like this: like her.

He smiles, though she cannot see him, though she does not even know he stands by the fence a few meters away.

There is no warning when that changes — when she turns and lifts her dark eyes from the white horse's mane to him and something deep, foreign, ancient, but not unwelcome, rings like a bell in his stomach and then settles down again, back into the bliss-

ful new calm he hadn't felt before she had noticed his presence.

His legs drive him forward, to her, without his permission. Her rosebud lips curve into a smile that could revive this infernal, dying season back into a mild and flowery spring.

It was no more than a flash of nonsensical colors and feelings, distant and untouchable. For a moment Drew had forgotten that she was standing in the middle of the Bizarre Bazaar, where vampires and steampunk princesses heaved in and out of the market stalls like blood pumping through a heart. For that moment there had been nothing else around her save for the dark-haired girl and the white steed. Now, in their stead, there was only a fair girl brushing her hand absently down the chest of a chestnut horse harnessed to an empty cart. There were no dark eyes or knowing smiles, no butterflies or warmth. They had all gone with whatever it was — déjà vu, perhaps — that Drew had felt.

The pocket watch hadn't. It was cool and heavy in her palm, engraved with the date, 1717, in a polished gold that could not have been its original gilding. The woman manning the antiques stall watched curiously — had been watching the whole time as she waited for Drew to pay.

She debated, glancing at the curling sticker on the back where the price had been scrawled in black pen. It was not so expensive for an antique, but it was not like Drew to waste her money, either. It surprised her just as much as the older woman when she pulled out her purse and paid with old, crumpled notes she had been saving for petrol.

"Bag?" the seller asked impatiently.

"No, thank you," Drew replied, putting both her purse and the watch in her small shoulder bag. "Do you happen to know anything about it?"

"Not really." She chewed on a piece of gum with little interest in Drew or anything else happening around her. "Only that it was repaired and restored about a decade ago."

"But it was originally made in 1717?"

The woman shrugged, raising an eyebrow. Drew supposed she was not her standard customer, what with the fact that she was only in her early twenties, for starters.

"So it suggests on the cover," the seller said.

Drew knew it would be no use to inquire further and nodded her thanks before wandering off to the next stall, her bag now a pocket watch heavier than it had been before. Still, she made sure to stand somewhere where the girl and the horse were in view, searching for glimpses of the memory — that was what it had felt like, at least: a memory of a dream, perhaps, or an old movie — that had taken her over at the very moment she had picked up the watch.

Nothing, now. Only a restless pull in her chest.

"Do you want to go for a ride later?"

Rusty had crept up on Drew and now stood beside her, a frown wrinkling her dark features. The rest of the band had opted to stay in the campervan, resting before tonight's performance in the pavilion that loomed on the cliffs above them. Drew was glad to be free of them after having spent weeks cramped in the Volkswagen.

"What?" Drew replied finally, the peace she had felt a moment ago shattering with the word. Too much chatter and chaos. Too many bodies brushing past her arm even though she had wandered out of the way of the main crowds. To distract herself, she stole Rusty's flask, wincing at the sugary bitterness of the tea she sipped. Lemon and honey — to protect her vocal cords, Rusty always insisted. Not quite the rock-and-roll lifestyle expected of her, but Drew supposed she should at least be glad that her bandmate wasn't drinking vodka at ten o'clock in the morning.

"Do you mind? I don't want your germs." Rusty snatched the flask back with a grave scowl and nodded to the horse and cart, to the fair-haired girl who looked nothing like she should have. "The horse. You were staring at it."

"Was I?" Drew blinked blankly and wandered to the next stall, inspecting the gemstones on the table with feigned interest. The cold, heavy amethyst was a comfort against her rough flesh, though the middle-aged man behind the table watched her warily. Drew pretended not to notice, pretended as though the very look did not make her feel like a criminal.

Rusty joined her, fingers dancing across smooth faces of moonstone and obsidian until they landed on a veiny cut of turquoise that matched the dyed tips of her otherwise brown hair. Other than the small splash of color, this morning she looked nothing like the lead vocalist of the unknown rock band Siren Whisper, with her freckled face bare of its usual smudged makeup and a knitted hat perched on her roughly chopped straight hair. Drew supposed she looked just as tame among the goth festival-goers, with her plain leather jacket and hair twisted into a bun, where it would not bother her.

"Oh my goodness, is that rock star Drew Dawson mingling with the commoners?" a high, excited voice called out above the chatter of the shoppers. Drew knew whom it belonged to immediately, but turned around anyway, a smile already spreading on her face.

It had only been a matter of time before he found her.

Ethan Moors pushed through witches and corpse brides to get to her, fanning his face in mock excitement. Drew laughed, falling into his outstretched arms as he reached her and allowing him — she would allow *only* him — to rock her back and forth excitedly.

"It's good to see you, my love."

"And you," she breathed into his ear before pulling away. He hadn't changed a bit since the last time she had seen him, a year or so ago, when he had visited her in Birmingham for a show. He blended in well with the rest of the town in his usual clothes: black lace shirt and long coat. His mop of raven hair was curled atop his head, stiff with hairspray, his hazel eyes brightened by the thin line of kohl around his lids. His lips and cheeks, though, were as pink as ever. "This is —"

"Rusty," he completed for her, offering an eager hand for Drew's bandmate to shake. Rusty did, hesitantly, eyeing Ethan as though he were another species entirely. "I know. I did my research."

"Rusty, this is Ethan," Drew said with a proud smile. "He's the one who invited us to play here."

"I am Drew's very own Simon Cowell." He nodded. "I discovered her at an open-mic night back in our university days."

"And then he spent another two years convincing me to audition for a band," Drew added dryly. She had almost forgotten about the gemstones in her hands. She put them down now, ignoring the glare of the seller as she stepped away from the glittering table of crystals.

"And here we are." He flourished to an invisible audience, his arm almost colliding with Rusty's face in the process so that she had to duck to avoid it. "Fame and fortune, all because of me."

Drew arched an eyebrow. "I wouldn't go that far." Though the show they were playing this afternoon was slightly bigger than those in the dingy bars they usually played in, the tiny coastal town wasn't quite Glastonbury, and people were hardly lining up to get their autographs — a fact that Drew did not find too devastating. She had always been happy to play her music to even a handful of people. In fact, the thought of today's crowd sent a shudder of nerves through her stomach.

"You'll see. You'll be begging for me to be your manager soon enough," Ethan promised, patting her shoulder confidently. "Anyway, I'm having a Halloween party tomorrow night after the last of the shows. I want you all there."

Drew hesitated, casting her gaze to Rusty in question. Rusty, still less than impressed with Ethan's bubbly disposition, shook her head subtly when her narrowed brown eyes locked on Drew's.

"Actually, we haven't been able to find a place to park the camper overnight," Drew said, receiving Rusty's message loud and clear. "We were going to get straight back on the road after the show."

"Oh, don't be ridiculous," Ethan scoffed, waving his hand dismissively to display a set of glinting silver rings: one for every finger. "I know a space with plenty of room for a camper."

Drew bit her lip, looking at Rusty again.

Rusty only sighed and sipped her tea. Hot

steam still curled out of the top. "I suppose we can stay for a few days."

Ethan clapped his hands like a performing seal. Drew almost winced on his behalf. "Perfect. I have a few things to do here, and then I'll show you where to park up."

"Great," Drew said.

"Perfect," Rusty mimicked beside her. If Ethan heard the sarcasm dripping from her tone, he did not show it. Instead he gathered Drew into a final hug before swaggering back into the crowd. It had already gotten busier as the sun rose higher in the sky, the smell of spices and smoky bacon wafting through the bazaar as food vendors joined the jewelry and vintage-clothes stalls around them.

"Be nice," Drew scolded Rusty, sauntering to the next stall, where a collection of dreamcatchers and incense was organized across the tables. "He's a good friend, and we wouldn't be here without him."

"We're not staying," Rusty replied, no longer so much as pretending to be interested in the goods being sold in front of her. "They won't agree to it."

"Then you can be the one to tell him." Drew grinned wryly and stole the flask again, the foul-tasting tea warming her empty, nervous stomach. She looked back only once, to where the girl and the horse had been standing. The cobblestones were empty now save for a tour guide directing the visitors this way and that.

For a moment Drew wondered if she had imagined the horse and cart, the girl who had had brown hair one moment and blonde the next. Then Rusty dragged her through the sheltered bazaar to a vendor selling pancakes and waffles, and any thought, any questions, vanished altogether.

Breakfast was what she needed. Breakfast would set her at ease — at least, that was what she told herself as she took a seat beneath a striped umbrella and looked up to the building atop the cliffs.

The building where, soon, her drumbeats would be echoing through an audience.

Two

"Your brother should be home by now." Amber's father scratched his salt-and-pepper beard, his figure casting a shadow onto Amber from where he sat on the cart above her. "Why don't you pop home and see if he's settling okay?"

Amber scowled in response, running an absent hand down Stoker's smooth muzzle to distract herself. The horse's glistening black eye watched her every move as though knowing, too, that checking on her brother was the last thing she wanted.

"He lived in that house for eighteen years, Dad," she sighed finally, adjusting Stoker's bridle. "I'm sure he's settled just fine."

"Maybe his girlfriend would like a tour of the town before it gets too busy," he suggested, never one to give up his faith that Amber would one day stop holding a grudge, even after all this time.

"Then Kit can give her one, can't he?" she retorted, giving Stoker a final pat down before stepping away from both him and her father. Ethan had named the horse after Bram Stoker himself in an attempt to keep the town's history — it had been featured in *Dracula* — alive, and though Amber wasn't usually a horse person, she had taken to him more than she would like to admit — had practically grown up with him. She only pitied that the poor thing would have to spend the day slogging the cart through the streets of Whitby, carrying visitors who had come to visit for the annual Halloween festival.

"Amber," he scolded, his tired eyes the same shade of gray as the clouds lingering on the horizon. Amber hated that just the way he said her name, just the way he looked at her, could summon that flicker of guilt in the pit of her stomach. "He's your brother. Sooner or later you're going to have to forgive him."

"Why?" Anger crackled in her rising voice. "He's only here once a year anyway. Twice, if we're lucky."

"Maybe he would come more often if you weren't so bloody stubborn," her father grumbled, gripping the horse's reins and shuffling on the bench. It was odd to see him sitting up there in his top hat and Victorian-style suit. Chauffeur was not his usual job, nor did he usually put any effort at all into what he wore — he never needed to on the fishing boat, unless he was hosting a trip. Still, he had not bothered to shave his scraggly beard or fasten the top button on his collar: his small rebellion, perhaps, for having been roped into this last-minute by Ethan.

Amber tutted at both his appearance and

his words, inspecting the large wheels of the cart to avoid his gaze. "So it's my fault, then?"

John only shook his head in defeat, sucking in an impatient breath before pulling his black gloves on. "Just go and see your brother, Amber. Please."

His abrupt dismissal might have had more of an impact if he were abandoning Amber by any other means than a horse and cart. He was not, though, and the steady rhythm of Stoker's trotting hooves was more welcoming than reproachful. Still, she glanced hesitantly across the River Esk, to where her own crooked little house sat behind the anchored fishing boats that bobbed on the water's surface.

Her father was right. She knew that, knew that she wasn't a child and could not continue to throw tantrums for the rest of her life because her brother had decided to leave this sinking little town in favor of a stable career in a big city. Still, she could not help the anger that crawled beneath her skin, even after three years of being used to his absence.

With a long, wavering sigh, she forced her legs in the opposite direction, to the sheltered bazaar, where already a myriad of stalls had opened and crowds had gathered around them. She would give it an hour or so before facing her brother. There were plenty of ways to keep herself busy until then.

∞∞∞

Though she had expected them, Amber still glowered at the sound of voices — one low, familiar, and another irritatingly high and sweet — as she stepped into the narrow hallway and stumbled over the two duffel bags piled beside the stray shoes on the trodden-down carpet.

"Dad, is that you?" her brother, Kit, called out as she shut the front door, putting an end to their conversation. When she turned around, she found her brother standing on the threshold of the kitchen, looking nothing like he had the last time she'd seen him — Christmas last year. He had still been wearing the ugly sweaters their grandmother always knitted for them, then, and hadn't cut his long, sandy curls yet. Now his hair was straight and short, and he wore a black turtleneck that made him look twice his age at first glance.

A soft "Oh" fell from his lips at the sight of Amber jiggling her set of house keys. She didn't bother to take off her coat or her hat, didn't bother to move at all as he stared gormlessly at her, the dark hallway saturated with silence. And then another set of footsteps approached behind him: Emily, Kit's girlfriend, peered over his shoulder on her tiptoes. Amber only blinked and pretended not to see her.

"Dad asked me to make sure you were settling in okay," she said to Kit, crossing her arms over her chest as though guarding the feelings simmering within.

"We are." Kit nodded. "Thank you."

"He's on horse-and-cart duty today," she explained, if only to fill the quiet. "He won't be back until dinner."

"And you?"

"I'm helping Ethan at the pavilion later on."

"Goodie!" Emily exclaimed, with so much enthusiasm that Amber almost jumped out of her skin. "I can't wait to see some of the bands."

"I didn't know you were into rock and metal." Amber raised an eyebrow, ignoring the daggers that Kit shot her. *Be nice*, she could hear him ordering through those narrowed eyes, so much like her own. They had both inherited the dull, icy blue from their mother. Perhaps that was just another reason why she couldn't look at Kit properly these days.

Emily shrugged. "Any excuse to dance." She smiled, hooking her arm through Kit's. "We were just going to put the kettle on if you fancied a cup of tea."

"No, thank you," Amber replied frostily, pushing past the two of them to get into the kitchen. She snatched her purse up from the table and shoved it in her bag. "I just came for this."

She paused at the kitchen window, a flash of orange catching her eye. An old Volkswagen camper sat on the dusty gravel drive by her father's shed, dark curtains drawn shut and stickers of skulls and roses littering the sides. "Do you own a campervan now?"

"God, no." Kit shuddered at the thought as he put the kettle on the stove, ducking his head to glance out the window. "It was there when we got here. Couldn't get onto the drive because of it, so we parked on the street round the corner. We thought maybe you were letting one of the bands stay."

"If we are, it's news to me," she muttered, placing her bag on the counter. "I'll sort it out."

Kit's expression turned wary with the anticipation of what was to come, of the wrath Amber was going to bring upon whoever it was that had decided to make her private driveway their new home. It was a big space for a small house, granted, but that was because her father used it when he needed to fix up his boat. It was certainly not made for lazy tourists in grotty little campervans who refused to pay for a hotel.

Amber stormed out the back door without another word, letting it swing on its hinges so aggressively that she would have to check later if she'd made a dent in the wall — the last thing she needed. The gravel crunched beneath her boots, quieting only when she came to a stop at the van and rapped forcefully on the window.

The sound of shuffling and whispers erupted from within, but there was no other sign of whoever was inside. She knocked again, this time so hard that the sting remained across her knuckles long after she'd let her hand fall back to her side. The black curtains twitched, a pair of dark eyes glaring out at her in the shadows. She raised her eyebrows, huffing impatiently and putting her hands on her hips before knocking a final time.

"All right, all right," a husky voice sighed. The door slid open with a low rumble, revealing a dark-haired girl in what looked to be black, starry pajamas. Three other girls sat on the floor behind her, squashed against mismatched furniture and musical instruments, but Amber's attention remained solely on the one in front of her. A look of surprise fluttered across the girl's features for only a moment before it was wiped away. Amber got that reaction from strangers often, what with the birthmark around her eye that made her feel like a panda. "Can I help you?"

"I certainly hope so," Amber bit back, brows arching at the girl's audacity. "This driveway isn't a campsite. It's a private driveway, meaning it belongs to me. You can't stay here."

"We were told it wasn't in use." The girl climbed out of the van, crossing her arms and frowning. Her skin was a dewy brown in the daylight, her hair a ruffled mass of inky-black waves that needed desperately to be tamed by a strong comb.

"By who?" Amber demanded.

"Ethan Moors," she answered, tilting her

head as though in question. "He said that you wouldn't mind if we stayed here for the weekend."

Ethan Moors. It wasn't one bit of a surprise that Ethan was offering out Amber's driveway as a free-for-all carpark. He had already roped her and her father into everything else this weekend. Ethan Moors was going to get an earful the next time Amber saw him.

Amber rolled her eyes. "Are you friends of his?"

"I am." The girl nodded, licking her lips in a way that drew Amber's attention straight to them. They were plump, heart-shaped, the kind that were made for deep-red lipstick and...

Amber dragged her gaze away when she realized she had been staring and lifted her eyes to find that Kit was still watching from the window, a steaming mug now in his hand. The glower returned to her face.

"We're playing at the pavilion this afternoon," she clarified.

"You're one of the bands?"

"Siren Whisper." She motioned behind her, where the group sat, looking bored. A brunette woman with blue-green highlights at the tips cast Amber an amused wave at the sudden attention. Amber had never heard of, nor seen, the band before, though she vaguely recalled Ethan talking about how he had booked an old friend's band a few months ago. Not that it made a difference. "Look, if it's really an issue, we can find another

18

place to park."

"You can find somewhere to park other than *my* drive?" Sarcasm laced Amber's words. "How considerate."

"All right." The girl threw her hands up in caution, backing away. "Fine. We'll be out of your hair in five minutes."

"Ethan's parents own a farm with plenty of space," Amber responded. "Tell him he can use his own property to house the homeless next time."

"Ouch," the blue-haired girl drawled from the van as the other climbed into the back. She swapped places with her, climbing out onto the gravel before sliding into the driver's seat. "I must admit, I like you more than that Ethan character." Her grin revealed a large gap between her two front teeth, but it was wiped away a moment later as she slammed the door shut and slid on her seatbelt.

"I won't save you a ticket to the show, then," the black-haired girl teased from the back of the van before slamming the door shut so loudly that Amber's ears were left ringing. The tires spun to life a moment later, flinging up gravel that caked Amber's black jeans in white powder.

She stepped away from the van, still glaring at it long after it disappeared, leaving her standing alone in the empty driveway.

Three

Drew twiddled her drumsticks nervously around her fingers as she paced the echoing corridor. Unsettling wails accompanied by the low, repetitive thud of bass floated from the main stage, distant — yet not distant enough to be able to tune the awful noise out.

Rusty seemed not to be affected by nerves at all. She sat cross-legged on the grimy floor, humming the words of their song to herself. Beside her, Zandra thrummed her dainty, calloused fingers across her frayed denim jeans as though playing invisible keys. Max, the bassist, was still touching up her makeup in the bathroom: no surprise there.

Drew puffed out a deep breath in an attempt to calm herself, letting her sticks tap the air with movements her muscles had sealed into their memory long ago. The silent beat was broken not a moment later when Ethan appeared at the top of the corridor, wearing even more jewelry and eyeliner than this morning, if it was possible.

"There they are," he crooned proudly. Drew assumed he was talking to himself until she saw a blonde girl — the blonde girl, she realized, from earlier. The one who had been petting the horse, and the one who had been incredibly assertive in her instruction to move the camper from her drive. "Siren Whisper, in the flesh. Wait —"

Ethan counted their heads, reaching three before he blanched. "Aren't there supposed to be four of you? Don't tell me one of you has already quit."

"I'm here!" Max called from the other end of the corridor, compact mirror still clutched in her hand as she stumbled toward them, distracted by her own vibrant reflection. Her pink hair had been backcombed into a fluffy mass, her eyeliner a dotted blue that trailed so far out from her lids that it was almost lost in her hairline.

Relieved, Ethan clutched a hand to his chest. "Oh, thank goodness. I thought I was going to have to fill in."

"I wouldn't wish you attempting to play a musical instrument on anyone," Drew retorted.

"That's because you haven't heard me play the ukulele yet." He waved off the insult and stepped aside so that the fair-haired girl was in full view. If she was embarrassed to be standing in front of the very four people she had insulted this morning, she did not show it. Her eyes were icy, one of them shrouded by a purple birthmark that escaped in splatters until it faded into freckles across her cheek and jaw. It had not fazed Drew earlier: a part of her had expected to see it there, had felt a familiar warmth spreading deep within her at the sight of it, one that she could not explain or understand. "This is my best friend, Amber. She's helping me out today."

Something in Drew's chest and stomach, something in her *bones*, sighed her name in relief — knowing. *Amber*. Drew had wondered what it would be all morning, and had also wondered why she still felt pleasantly familiar even after the less than pleasant conversation. At least now she knew her name.

"Oh." Rusty laughed, vaulting herself up from the floor and wiping down her dirty palms. "We've met Amber."

"She's quite lovely," Zandra added with a crooked smirk brightening her wan face. Her short hair stuck out at every angle.

At their responses, Ethan cast Amber a confused glance.

Amber only glared at him. "Perhaps you should stop telling people to park their grotty campervans on my property instead of your own."

"Excuse me?" Drew raised an eyebrow. "Edna is *not* grotty, thank you very much."

"Edna?" Amber repeated, incredulous.

"Edna the Camper," Max confirmed. "Named after my grandmother."

"Of course. Did Edna the grandmother also have four wheels and an engine?"

Drew swallowed her laugh, catching the way that Max scowled at Amber across the corridor as she smacked her flame-orange lips together a final time and put the mirror away.

"Anyway." Ethan distracted them all quickly. "Amber and I are taking a few friends on a ghost walk tonight, if you're up for it. What do you think?"

"I think that we're not seven, but thank you for the offer." Rusty smiled falsely, tugging at her nose ring as though afraid she might lose the thick metal hoop onstage.

Ethan overlooked the mockery in Rusty's tone, turning his attention to Drew. His dark eyes were pleading, eyeliner smudged beneath. Beside him, Amber looked less than impressed at the prospect of spending time with them. Still, Drew sighed and nodded. She had not seen Ethan for so long that it wouldn't feel right to pass up the little time they had together — even if Rusty and the rest of the band didn't care for his antics. "I suppose it could be fun."

"It *will* be fun," he assured her, pausing and holding a finger up to silence everybody when the stage noise began to fade out. "I think it's almost time."

Drew's heart began to hammer, but she shook the nerves from her limbs and followed the band down the corridor. Amber had somehow ended up beside her, her arm brushing against Drew's. As though sensing it too, she took a step away as they emerged backstage. It was dark save for the computer screens of the sound and light technicians: the type of dark that felt smothering and raw.

Despite her nerves, it was the type of dark that Drew loved.

"Good luck," Amber murmured beside her, so quiet that Drew was the only one to hear. Perhaps she had intended it that way. Drew smiled down at her in appreciation despite the hostility still rolling from the shorter girl and then came to a sudden halt.

Another wave of déjà vu took Drew hostage, rattling her around in its strange, icy grip. *Did* she know Amber? Perhaps Ethan had introduced them at university, and Drew had just been too drunk to remember — but how could she ever have forgotten her when she was so … *her*?

This did not feel like the first time Drew had stood in the stifling darkness with Amber, and the thought, the feeling, the shadows, swallowed her whole.

∞∞∞

Beads and fringe dresses glint silver in the darkness, but not hers. Hers is a vibrant red: the color of the devil, and of fire; the color of blood. She places his hand on her waist invitingly, and he keeps it there, not daring to take it away, to let her go. They hide in a quiet corner where the music barely reaches them. They are safe in the shadows. An underground bar full of people, and yet nobody exists but her and her wine-stained lips and the delicate, pointy fingernail tracing spirals into his arm.

"You'll be mine by the end of the night," she whispers into his ear. He bows his head so he can hear her better.

"Will I?" He tries to hide his blush behind his white collar. He is an angel tonight, with wings strapped to his shoulders. She is the devil, in a crimson dress and heels that could take off his toe if she accidentally stood on his foot. But nothing she does is by accident, and he knows that.

She nods, hands lying flat against his chest so that the watch in his breast pocket presses into his skin. He no longer feels it tick — whether because it has stopped or because it is too faint in comparison to the pumping of his own heart, he doesn't know.

"Yes."

"And if I run away?" There's a darkness in his tone that wasn't there before, a darkness that he knows is there for a reason — a reason he cannot remember.

"Good luck trying." She smirks. "I'll always find you."

It is a promise he is certain she will keep.

Four

Amber had never truly watched somebody play the drums before, had never acknowledged the hard work that went into moving the sticks at just the right time with just the right amount of force. She couldn't take her eyes off the drummer of Siren Whisper now from where she stood in the wings, clutching the red velvet curtain to keep herself hidden from the audience.

Sweat was beginning to pool in the hollow of the drummer's neck, her entire body taut with unspent energy — so much so that every part of her seemed to tremble: her leg on the pedal, her fingers never stopping for a beat, her head nodding to the music, even. Her teeth were sunk into her bottom lip, eyes half-closed as she mouthed the words of their song.

The music wasn't so bad either, if Amber put her pride aside for long enough to admit it. It wasn't quite as heavy or piercing as the other bands here this weekend, the lead singer's voice gravelly and dream-like, though still able to be heard over the low, thick instrumentals. Amber stood on her tiptoes to gauge the audience's reaction. Most seemed to be enjoying them, nodding their heads or swaying, those who had most likely been drinking all day dancing with their friends in a world of their own. Amber half-wished she could join in. She couldn't remember the last time she had felt so free, the last time she had let her hair down and danced to deafening music without care for anything else around her.

Ethan nudged her side, the corner of his mouth raised smugly. "Not bad, are they?"

"I've heard worse bands perform over the years." Amber shrugged. "They're still staying on your farm, though."

Ethan rolled his eyes. "Would it kill you to stop being so moody for a weekend?"

"Yes," she retorted through gritted teeth, though something in her sank. She didn't mean to be moody or unapproachable — wished, even, she could be more like Ethan, who found joy in every second of his life and hopped about the town with an energy and bubbliness that exhausted her just to watch. "It would."

"All right," Ethan huffed, pinching her elbow and tugging her away from the stage and the curtains, away from the blinding lights. "What's up with you? You've been acting even more..." He searched, cautiously, for the right word. "Standoffish than usual."

"Nothing," Amber replied blankly, looking anywhere but at him. When his stony expression remained unsatisfied, unconvinced, she sighed and slumped against the back wall. "My brother is in town, that's all. He's staying with us for the weekend. And he brought his new girlfriend."

"Kit's in town?" Excitement lifted in Ethan's voice. "Amazing. Tell him to come to the party tomorrow night."

It seemed he had already forgotten Amber's foul mood, because he wandered back to the curtain without another word, knees bobbing in time with the music.

Amber shook her head. She was beginning to get a headache, and the music pulsed in her chest from the amp beside her in a way that made it difficult to catch her breath. She would rather be anywhere but here, so she slid out of the wings without a goodbye, leaving Ethan to watch the band alone.

Five

Drew always felt like a live wire after playing a set, her arms aching and restless from hitting the drums with unchecked force and electricity flooding through her, generated from the cheers and applause they received. Tonight was no different as the band ambled back into town with Ethan. The audience had loved them. Drew had expected it to be a quiet show like most of their others, especially with it only being mid-afternoon — most of the popular bands wouldn't be on until later — but it hadn't been at all. In fact, she had never felt such a rush.

The only thing that had dulled it ever so slightly was the fact that Amber had disappeared at some point. She hadn't wanted to ask Ethan where she was, knowing it would be strange if she did, considering that they barely knew one another. It didn't feel that way, though, not really. She still hadn't figured out why that was, and it had played on her mind with every beat of her drumstick against the tight skin, every lyric she sang along to.

She sucked in a deep breath to distract herself, closing her eyes as the cool afternoon air dried the sweat from her face. Her drumsticks still jutted from the back pocket of her jeans; she could never bring herself to part with them after all they did for her when she was onstage.

The town was flooded with people now, and more white-and-red gazebos filled the spaces that had been empty around the bazaar this morning. Drew paused for a moment, taking it in: the costumed crowds, the chatter and the playfulness she didn't see often anymore, the smell of fried onions and fresh donuts, and beneath that, the salt coming off the sea and the fish that had been caught this morning. It wasn't often that she visited coastal towns, but this one she would like to come back to when it was quieter. She could imagine it well on a lazy summer's day, with fishing boats idling in the harbor and the sea lapping peacefully below the pier.

Yes, she would like to come back at some point, found comfort in the idea that she might.

"Earth to Drew," Rusty called. The others were at the bottom of the hill, waiting impatiently for Drew to catch up with them. She did, her knees almost giving out as she took the last few steps onto the cobblestones.

A girl with a familiar head of blonde hair stood at the railings, her back to them. Drew faltered, eyebrows furrowing. Why was she standing alone? And why was that feeling still there — the heavy, unsettling one that twisted and danced in the bottom of her stomach, singing Amber's name?

Ethan followed Drew's gaze before she could find out the answer to the first question. "Amber." He sang her name too, though not quite in the same key. "I wondered where you'd got to."

She turned around, her lips pressed into a thin line. "Needed fresh air," she explained, wiping her hands on her jeans as she approached them. She met Drew's eyes for only a moment: they were glassy from the cold — a bright, electrifyingly pale blue. The color of Drew's exhilaration.

"Were we that awful?" Drew was only half joking. She thrust her hands into the pockets of her jacket, the cold reaching her now that the adrenaline from the show was wearing off. Her fingers found the pocket watch and curled around it instinctively.

Amber shrugged. "Not bad."

Ethan gasped, linking arms with Max and pointing at a stall. "Look at those shirts." Drew did: they were almost identical in their frills and lace to the one that Ethan currently wore. "I need them. All of them."

"They have dresses, too." Max matched his own excitement, and the two of them ran off without giving the rest of them a second glance.

Rusty scowled at their backs. "I need food. Are you coming?"

Zandra nodded eagerly, placing a hand on her tiny stomach. "I could eat a scabby horse."

"Drew?"

Drew didn't know why she glanced at Amber in question, didn't know why her feet felt planted to the spot even as Zandra and Rusty began to walk backward in the direction of the food trucks. Though the sharp smell of spices and herbs caused Drew's mouth to water, she did not feel like going with them yet. She liked the peace she felt standing here, with Amber, by the water.

"I'm good. I'll catch up with you later."

Rusty's suspicious glance flitted between Drew and Amber. Then she shrugged. "Suit yourself," she said before she and Zandra merged into the crowd.

Amber did not deign to so much as ask why Drew had decided to stay, instead returning to the position she had been in before, with her elbows resting against the bars that separated them from the river. Drew joined her with a sigh, veins abuzz with both the chaos and the peace she had been subjected to — was still being subjected to. The sun was already lowering behind the bare bones of the old abbey at the top of the cliffs, the day cooling off as the threat of night began to brew.

"It lights up at night," Amber said, following her focus to the cliffs. "Only for this week, though."

"It's pretty." Drew nodded gently. "Have you lived here your whole life?"

"Yep," she replied, popping the *P*. "Lucky me."

"You are," Drew agreed, though she couldn't

be sure if Amber was being sarcastic. "I always stuck to the cities before Edna."

"Edna the Camper." For the first time since Drew had met her this morning, Amber's lips curled into a subtle, appreciative smile. Something small fluttered in Drew at the sight of it. "Doesn't it get claustrophobic, living on top of each other like that?"

"God, yes," Drew admitted. "We're always bickering. I try to stay out of it where I can."

"I wouldn't manage. I like my own space."

"I gathered." Drew's fingers tapped idly on the bars as she straightened. "So how did somebody like you become friends with somebody like Ethan?"

Amber's expression turned stony, and Drew knew immediately she had said the wrong thing. She did not shrink back, though, unafraid of the anger simmering behind Amber's icy eyes. She was too fascinated by her, too busy trying to understand her. *Who is she?*

"Meaning?" Amber snapped.

"Just that Ethan can be a real pain in the arse if you're around him long enough," she said carefully, shielding her eyes with her hand against the low sun, "and you don't seem to put up with most people's..." She searched for the word but couldn't find one, so she left the sentence to trail off and wished she had never started it to begin with.

Amber's jaw clenched. She looked over to

where Ethan still stood, holding blouses to his torso while Max inspected the material and the fit for him. It was no surprise that the two were already getting along, especially where it involved fashion.

"Ethan is Ethan," Amber said finally. "You put up with him because you wouldn't have him any other way. Besides, we've been friends since we were kids. He's always been part of my life."

Drew nodded, biting the inside of her cheek as she twisted to look back at the bazaar. One of the tents closest was decorated with fairy lights and red and gold stripes, half concealed by smoke curling from one of the food trucks beside it. The sign on the front read "Palm Readings and Tarot Cards" in swirled calligraphy. Drew had never thought of being read by a medium before, and was not even sure she believed in any of it, but she was drawn to the tent, drawn to the way the curtain waved in the slight breeze and to the stars and crescent moons decorating the sign.

"Drew!" Ethan's shout pulled her attention away from the tent and away from Amber. He was displaying a black velvet dress that was, admittedly, something Drew could see herself wearing, especially as the weather was turning and her current clothes were no longer protecting her from the brisk afternoons.

"Are you coming?" she asked Amber.

Amber hesitated, her gaze swaying across the river and then back again before she finally sighed. "I suppose."

Gladness twitched on Drew's lips. She liked being in Amber's company. She just didn't quite know why.

Six

Amber grimaced as she tried to shut the door as quietly as possible — and failed. The hinges were too old, too used, to do anything other than shriek at her, and the sound was followed soon after by her name being called from the kitchen.

"Amber?"

It was her father who waited for her this time, though Kit and Emily sat on either side of him at the dinner table. John no longer wore his black suit or top hat, already having reverted back to his threadbare sweater. She had pleaded with him to throw the tatty thing away a hundred times now, and still he could not part with it.

"Just in time to help me make dinner."

"I can't." She shrugged off her coat and hung it on the hook by the door. "I told Ethan I'd meet him later for the ghost walk."

"You do that every year. You can sit and have a meal with your family tonight." John dismissed her with a wave, the chair squealing beneath him as he stood. He was a tall man, his bones packed with thick, corded muscle even in middle age. Amber had certainly not inherited those genes. Still, she did not waver in her resolve as he crouched to pull pots and pans out from the cupboard beneath the sink.

"I sit and have a meal with my family every other night of the year," she snapped, ignoring the way that Emily shrank in her chair. Kit winced at her side. "The problem is that the only family here to witness it is you."

"Amber," John chided with an exhausted sigh, running his rough hands across his face impatiently.

"Oh, give it a rest, Amber," Kit snarled, standing up to match his father's height. A house divided, with Amber standing alone by the door as the two men across from her glowered — as though she were the one who had left. As though she were the one who had betrayed everybody. It made her sick. "Enough's enough. We can't do this forever."

She glared at Kit, and then at her father.

"I won't be here for dinner" was all she said before running up the stairs and retreating to her attic bedroom. She could have moved downstairs into her brother's room as her father had suggested when Kit had moved out, but this had always been hers. She liked being able to see the sky when she lay in bed, liked the way the roof curved above her and made her feel enclosed, safe.

She wished she could take a moment to revel in it now, but she didn't have the time. Instead she rifled through her wardrobe for a thick sweater and some thermals. The night had already turned bitter with the sunset outside, and she had spent enough nights like this one shivering before they had even reached the first attraction.

A knock from the bottom of the stairs stopped her before she could start to undress. She knew without looking who it would be, and took to plaiting her hair rather than inviting him up. The sound of Kit's footsteps, heavy on the old wood, creaked with his weight anyway, and she glimpsed him in the mirror of her vanity as she battled to tie her short hair into two braids. His face was flushed, frustration glittering in his eyes.

"Are you going to hate me forever, Amber?"

The sadness in his voice caused her heart to stutter. He tried desperately to meet her eye in the mirror. She did not let him, keeping her gaze cast down.

"I don't hate you," she answered nonchalantly, applying a quick layer of mascara to her fair eyelashes if only for something to do. It wasn't as though she wore makeup that often, but it took her attention from Kit. It was clear from the way he shifted on the stairwell that it aggravated him.

"You resent me," he murmured. "For leaving."

"Maybe."

"I understand. I do." He took a step toward her, knuckles turning white where he gripped the old wooden banister. "You feel as though I've betrayed you and Dad."

Amber sighed and threw her mascara down

before turning to face him. "You and me… we're all he has now."

"That doesn't mean we have to stop living our life. We deserve better than that, and he would never ask us to stay for him." He was brave enough now to sit on her old, lumpy mattress, his hands steepled together on his lap.

"That's the problem. He'd never ask, but it's what he wants."

"Is it what *you* want?"

"Yes." No hesitation. This town was her home, this way of life the only one she could imagine chasing for the rest of her own life, just as her mother had before she'd died. "I like fishing."

"Okay, fine." The way he always managed to keep himself calm and composed, steady, only made her angrier. "Why does it have to be what I want, too?"

"Because." She stuttered, cheeks prickling with heat. "We're your family. We're all he has."

She was aware that she sounded like a broken record. She had spent sleepless nights imagining having this conversation with her brother, and she hated that now, when she finally had the chance, the words were not coming out right.

Kit raised his eyebrows and leaned back on his hands. In so many ways, he was still the boy she had grown up with, irritating her when she had wanted to be alone and giving her that same disbelieving look. Yet his raincoats had been swapped for blazers, his plain, hole-infested tees for fancy button-up shirts. "Do you honestly expect me to stay here for the rest of my life, even when it doesn't make me happy?"

Amber swallowed and stood up, searching the bottom of her wardrobe for some boots. She found some too quickly. "He gets lonely without you."

"He has you."

"You and I both know I'm terrible company," she muttered.

"Only when you want to be."

She rolled her eyes at that, at all of it. Deep down, she could not blame Kit for leaving, but if he knew what it was like without him here, with pictures of her mother's ghost hanging on every wall and meals eaten in silence in a dark kitchen… wouldn't he be angry, too?

Of course she wanted him to be happy. She just wished he could be happy *here*.

"I wish you would come to visit me in Edinburgh," he admitted quietly, eyes cast down to his feet. "Maybe then you would understand."

"I hate cities," she replied. "I don't have time for this now, Kit. I need to get ready."

"Fine." His shoulders slumped in defeat as he stood, his trousers crinkled. "You know, I would support you no matter how you chose to live your life. So would Mum. I wish you would do the same for me."

Amber turned her back to him as the words landed their heavy blow. She shut her eyes against the pain and the guilt, against all of it. She knew that the reason they hurt so much was because they were true. Her mother had always encouraged her to do everything and anything, had never made either of them feel as though they had to keep the family business alive or keep the house afloat, despite how much she had invested into it for that very reason. She would have despised Amber's behavior if she saw her now, pushing away her brother the way she was.

But Amber couldn't help the way she felt, couldn't help how much it still hurt not to have both her brother and mother here, knowing that he had found another home in another place that was nothing like this one.

So she let him walk away, let him leave her where only the echo of his words filled the aching silence.

The silence was where she lived now, anyway.

Seven

The night had turned cold too quickly, and it meant that the numbers for the ghost walk had dwindled. Rusty and Zandra had already opted to find a pub rather than spend their evening "freezing their tits off," as Rusty had so eloquently put it. That left only Drew, Max, and Ethan, plus a few strangers. They waited beneath a stone archway for Amber to make her appearance, shivering against the brisk wind blowing in from the sea. The bazaar was closing down in the heart of the town for the night, the lights blinking into darkness in staggered intervals until the only ones came from the houses and inns surrounding them. The moon was full and bright, though, so that even if there were no streetlights, it wouldn't be so pitch black that Drew couldn't see a thing.

"Maybe she's not coming," Drew suggested, dancing on the spot to keep warm. She already wished that she had followed Rusty and Zandra, could imagine the golden, stale warmth of an old pub welcoming her in from the cold.

"She's coming," Ethan countered defensively, tucking his hands into his pockets. Even he had abandoned his fancy shirts in favor of a large turtleneck that was mostly covered by a thick black scarf and coat. "We do this every year."

"Isn't that her?" Max nodded to something behind Drew. She turned, sighing in relief when she caught a glimpse of a small silhouette making her way up the crumbling steps. Amber's features sharpened as she floated into the orange glow of the streetlights. Her nose was already red from the cold, her eyes glazed and her hair covered by a bobble hat that jiggled atop her head as she walked.

"Sorry." Amber's breath curled into the night, her breaths ragged as though she had run here. "I got held up at home."

"Better late than never," Ethan remarked, bouncing to life as Amber reached them.

She stopped, gauging the few people who had joined aside from Ethan, Max, and Drew. "Is this all there is?"

Ethan shrugged. "Looks that way."

Amber blinked reluctantly. Drew couldn't help but gaze at her when she wasn't looking, at the way her watery eyes shone and the way she bit her chapped bottom lip. Everything she did, every mannerism and look, was so familiar that Drew's stomach twisted in response. "Is there any point, then?"

The disappointment that Drew felt at cutting the night short was unexpected, especially when she had been fantasizing about beer and warmth only a moment ago. "Come on," she moaned. "I want to see some ghosts."

"You're not backing out on me now," Ethan agreed, pulling Amber by the elbow. "It's tradition."

"Okay," Amber sighed in resignation. "Let's go."

They did, footsteps echoing as they passed through the damp tunnel. Another set of old, steep steps loomed over them on the other side, the abbey ruins awaiting them at the top of the hill. The stone skeleton had been lit with floor lights, just as Amber had said earlier, and the eerie green glow bled into the night sky. Whatever the old building had once housed within was gone, replaced by shadows that dripped through the unglazed windows. The full moon waned above, gray, wispy clouds lingering across its silver light. [1][2][3]

"As most of you know, part of Bram Stoker's *Dracula* was set here in Whitby," Amber began, standing on the first step so that she was high enough to be seen by the strangers at the back of the group. It was clear from the way her voice droned monotonously that she had made this speech more than a few times. "What you might not know is that other stories were born here, too. Ghost stories."

Ethan let out an enthusiastic wail to mimic a ghost, his long fingers crawling up Drew's arms like spider legs. She slapped him away, suppressing a laugh. Amber ignored the interaction and continued.

"On your walk up the hundred and ninety-nine steps to the abbey, you might be unlucky enough to hear a howl close by. Rumor has it that a beast haunts the Yorkshire Moors, ravaging farmers' livestock. If you do hear it, I'd advise you run: you're its next meal."

Anxious mutters erupted behind Drew, but she only grinned at the adrenaline surging through her. She relished the fear she felt whenever she watched a horror movie or read a ghost story. Even Amber's voice had darkened, as though she, too, couldn't help but invest herself in the tale.

"Let's go." She motioned up the steps with a nod, and Ethan and Max passed her as they began to climb. Drew followed, falling into step with Amber. Perhaps now was as good a time as any to figure out why she was so familiar, and why that familiarity was gnawing constantly at her and had been since the moment she'd seen her with the horse this morning.

"Have we met before?" she asked, wincing at her own bluntness. Climbing the steps was already becoming a labored, monotonous process of putting one foot in front of the other. Behind her, the others huffed as the movement and cold stole their breaths from their chest. Though they were a few steps behind, they might as well have been breathing in Drew's ear, and she gritted her teeth against the incessant sound.

"Several times," Amber deadpanned. "You were parked on my drive this morning."

"No, I know that." Drew laughed, though Amber didn't seem to be joking. "I mean before today."

"Hush," she scolded, a lightness in her tone that Drew hadn't expected. Behind her, the hills yawned out, vast and infinite. "You'll miss the howl."

"Right, sorry." Drew smirked, glancing at her from the corner of her eye. Amber's own mouth curved at the corner in amusement, her birthmark nothing more than a shadow on her pale face now. It was clear from the way she teased that she didn't believe in any of it, but Drew couldn't help but wonder at the sudden sound of a distant yelp traveling across the farmland. "Is that it?"

"Perhaps," Amber said. "Or perhaps it's the chihuahua that lives on Newton Street."

"Who knows?" A breathless chuckle fell out of Drew. Her legs were burning from all of the climbing, but the movement was keeping her warm, and she was thankful, at least, for that.

"No, though," Amber answered, casting her a quick, suspicious look. "We haven't met before. Why do you ask?"

"You just seem familiar." It felt silly to even say it — to give the strange, throbbing sensation that had bothered her all day any attention at all. "I don't know."

"Nope." Amber came to a stop on the step above Drew. The path forked off on one side to an old church whose shape looked more like a medieval fortress. Crooked gravestones had sunken into the soil in front of it, the ground wrapped in long, distorted shadows. Drew suppressed a shudder. No matter how much she loved horror, graveyards always awoke something ancient and bleak in her, especially when she thought of the abandoned bones rotting beneath the headstones.

"This is the Church of St. Mary. The graveyard is mentioned in *Dracula*, but more interesting than that is the tale of the phantom coach," Amber explained, guiding them through an old rusted gate and into the graveyard. It felt wrong to be here, using a place of rest to tell stories of spirits. Ice pooled in Drew's stomach. "It's said that if you stand here on a night like tonight, with the full moon illuminating your way, you might just hear the sound of horse hooves. If you're lucky, you might even catch a glimpse of the carriage and the coachman himself outside the church doors."

The unease sifting through the other tourists was palpable as they murmured and squirmed. Unease shifted in Drew as Amber guided them through the yard, weaving between crumbling gravestones and uneven ground. Ethan and Max were already ahead of them, messing around like children by the old church.

"Have you ever heard it?" Drew asked, if only to fill the unsettling silence.

"No," Amber replied, "but others have claimed to. My brother would never come up here, even now. He said he saw the horses once when he was a kid."

"Interesting," Drew murmured, glad when they were finally well away from the graves, the dead, the past. The church was not much more of a comfort, with the stained glass casting criss-cross silhouettes onto the grass. Behind, Drew could just make out the pointed arches of the abbey's half-walls piercing the night. "So what is it you do when you're not doing… this?"

"I catch fish." She leaned against the stone wall guarding the graveyard, burying her face into her scarf so that she was only half visible. "If you go to any restaurants this weekend, you might very well eat the cod I caught. Lucky you."

Drew raised her eyebrows, impressed. "I didn't have you down as an angler."

Amber shrugged, crossing her legs and rubbing her hands together to generate warmth. "It's a family business. My mum and dad taught me when I was young and it just stuck."

"Do you enjoy it?"

"I do." There was no uncertainty, no beat where she had to think about it — not like when Drew was asked the same question about drumming, and still had not gotten used to the answer being *yes*. "It's peaceful. I like being in my little boat away from everyone else."

"You're not a people person," Drew said wryly.

"What gave me away?"

"Good guess," Drew teased, perching beside her on the wall. "It definitely has nothing to do with how unapproachable and intimidating you are."

Amber's smile wavered for only a moment, and then she had a finger to her lips, shushing. Drew's brows knitted together as she listened. The wind howled through the dying trees, the crisp leaves rustling and scattering onto the ground. Even from here, the low music floated across the town from the pavilion, where bands still played into the night.

And beneath all of that, hooves pounding against stone.

Drew paled at the sight of the carriage being pulled along by the chestnut horse from earlier — not because she believed in the phantom coachman, but because her gut was beginning to churn again.

Because she had seen this before, in another place, another time.

Because it was happening again.

Their withered coachman gripping the reins, the horses haul the carriage to a stop beside the curb of a sunken path, where the elegant architecture of the old building carries light and music and ballgowns.

The coach door swings open. The passenger is already wearing his mask, wolf-shaped, with pointed ears made of bronze and a muzzle jutting out over his nose and mouth. The man standing by in the shadows glimpses only light eyes and a full, dimpled smile that makes him question everything he had been wishing for tonight. Just that smile changes everything.

But the masked man doesn't notice him standing alone, away from the lamplight and the crowds. He walks into the ballroom with his gloved hands locked in the grip of a dainty woman wearing too much tulle. She is masked too, but, even when half concealed by lace, he can tell she is beautiful.

No wonder the passenger does not notice the admirer he has acquired at first sight. No wonder he sees only his escort as he disappears into the throng of champagne-sipping, tuxedo-wearing guests.

No wonder.

Eight

Stoker was a tall, towering shadow at the top of the hill. Ethan's father sat in the cart behind, as he always did, to scare the tourists into thinking the phantom coachman was real.

Beside Amber, Drew had stilled completely. Even in the dark, she was pale save for the cluster of beauty spots that danced around her jaw and crawled into her scarf. Amber hadn't noticed them before tonight, but somehow she had known they were there. She had lied, too, in pretending that Drew wasn't familiar, though she was sure they hadn't met before. Perhaps it was just that Ethan had told her so many stories about the drummer that Amber felt as though she already knew her.

"Ethan's father," Amber reassured her when Drew caught her breath. Ethan and Max were petting Stoker now, the ghost tour forgotten and abandoned. *Good.* Tiredness gnawed at Amber, and she was cold. The sooner she could go home, the better.

Drew didn't reply, did not even appear to have heard her. Her eyes, near black but bright in the way they gleamed, were dazed and far away, somewhere that Amber couldn't reach.

"Drew?" she asked, frowning.

Drew blinked, tears gathering from the biting cold, and looked at Amber with an expression she couldn't decipher. It was wiped away before Amber could even begin to, replaced by a false glimmer of a smile.

"Sorry," Drew apologized, standing up. She was much taller than Amber, and her hips much wider. Amber demanded attention with her attitude, but Drew didn't have to do that; her curves and height already did it for her, and when she played the drums...

Amber still thought of the way she had played those drums, of the sweat dripping down her golden skin and the strained faces she had pulled as though it were the most precise art in the world.

If Drew thought of Amber nearly as much, she didn't show it. "I'm going to catch up with Max and Ethan," she excused herself, arms tightening around her torso. She practically ran away from Amber, away from the moment she'd thought they were having.

Not that Amber cared. Not that she wanted to talk more to Drew, to understand what she was thinking when those dark eyes devoured her with a hidden flame every so often. No, she felt nothing. And even if that was a lie, it didn't matter. Drew was just passing through. She was just a drummer in a band.

If she said it enough times, perhaps Amber

would convince herself that any of it was true.

Nine

He does not know who he is, but he knows her — even if he has never seen her before in his life, he knows her. Would know her anywhere. That much he is sure of.

She hasn't noticed him standing in the clearing. She never does. Hums escape her as she washes off-white linen in the lake, droplets of water rolling down her brown arms and into the sleeves of her dress. She is beautiful: her skin, eyes, hair, all the color of the earth. He had never believed his brother's stories of fairies and nymphs, but that changes now, when he hears her lilting melody and watches the way her lips curve upward in a private smile, as though she is so at peace here by this little forgotten lake. The silence does not scare her, and because of that, it does not scare him either.

He takes a step, and something hard is kicked from under his boot. A stone — no, it glints in the dappled sunlight. Something made of gold.

He picks it up, opens it. A pocket watch, the hands on half past ten. Hers?

Twigs snap beneath his boots as he shifts, and she lifts her head with all the swiftness of a fox sensing a predator in its woods. One half of her face lives in permanent shadow, a cloud of darkness staining

the socket of her eye and dribbling down her cheek.
Beautiful.

*He lifts his hands up in caution, afraid that
she will run, though that would be ridiculous. He is
just a boy, just a traveler. She seems to sense it, eyes
narrowing into curiosity as she lifts her hands from
the water and shakes them dry.*

*"You must live on the farm back there," he
says, accent thick — Irish.*

*"Yes, I do," she replies simply, standing and
wiping her hands down on an old, tatty apron tied
around her waist. "Why?"*

*"My brother and I have been looking for the
owners all morning."*

*She tilts her head, curls dancing across her face
with the wind. "My family are down in the village,
preparing for the Samhain festivities tonight."*

*"Ah." He nods. Somehow he is closer to her
now, with only a pool of water separating them.
Golden leaves have floated to the surface, and the
rest of the clearing, too, is afire with autumn's kiss.
A waterfall burbles across the lake, washing away
the clinging moss that summer has left behind on the
rocks. "We were wondering if perhaps you would take
in two travelers for a night or two. The horses need
rest and we could do with a decent place to sleep our-
selves."*

*She hesitates, shielding her eyes against the
low sun. "Who is 'we'?"*

*"My brother and me." He is closer still, so close
that he could touch her if he reached out. His boots*

sink into the banks of the lake, the smell of the earth giving him a respite, a stillness, he has not felt in days, weeks. "We're happy to rest in your stables with our horses if there are no rooms in your cottage. And of course we'll pay full price."

Her round, dark eyes remain guarded. "You'll get no peace here tonight. The villagers will be coming soon with their ale and their music and their dancing. We're having a bonfire."

"It won't be a problem." He keeps his tone light, though everything inside of him screams to do more, to be *more for her. He wants her to look at him and see him, to ask him what he wants to ask her:* have we met before? *"We're plenty used to bedlam."*

She fills a bucket beside her up with water and slings the linens over her shoulder. He feels a fool for standing in this clearing, letting his heart bleed for a stranger while she will not give him a second look.

"I'd imagine that my mother has already taken in a few of them for the night, so the rooms will be full. There will be tents outside, though, if that's any use."

He forces a smile. "Tents will do just fine. Thank you."

"Your name?" Her eyes lift, and he shivers.

"Shay."

"Shay," she repeats, and where it had been a simple syllable before, it is now the sound of the wind singing through the trees and the water splashing against the rocks. "I'm Aishling."

"It's nice to meet you, Aishling," he says, and means it. He has almost forgotten about the pocket

watch in his hand, only remembers it when he goes to grab the bucket from her with a chivalry he has never bothered to practice before. "I found this on the ground earlier." He holds it out, lets her examine it. She does, with little interest. "Is it yours?"

"I've never seen it before," she replies with a frown.

"It's broken anyway." He shrugs and slides it into his breast pocket before taking the bucket from her as carefully as his clumsy hands will allow. All the while, his heart whispers:

Aishling.

Aishling.

Aishling.

A song he cannot shake from his head as they venture back into the bramble and trees.

The dream Drew had had last night was already crumbling into faded images and shards of words that did not make sense to her anymore. She had woken up with the scent of the damp earth still in her nose and the taste of an Irish name still on her lips. The sun had been rising, slithering through the blackout curtains of the camper in a strip of pale amber, so she had sneaked out without waking the others and let Ethan drive her into town. He was busy again today, he said, at the pavilion, and she was glad. She wanted to be alone with the sea, had stood at the pier, swathed in the blanket of dawn's golden glow while tossing the pocket watch between her hands. The sea had been a calm beast curling around the rocks beneath, setting her in a trance that only the arrival of the day had broken. Drew had never been so close to the ocean before, had never tasted it on her lips the way she could now. She had thought it would be enough to wash away the unease that had followed her around for over a day.

It hadn't.

She was making her way back up the cobbled roads when everything began to stir to life again, the shops opening their shutters and the stall owners setting up the bazaar for another day of sales and festivities. Drew wasn't quite ready for the chaos yet. In fact, the perfumed incense floating off one of the tables was making her nauseous. She was thinking about heading back to Ethan's farm and catching up on lost sleep when she reached the docks.

The smell of freshly caught fish dragged the exhaustion straight out of her. It was quiet save for Amber, who was tying up her boat.[4] She would have been unrecognizable had she not been wearing the same mustard-yellow hat she had been last night, her short hair still twisted into two braids — though it was trying to escape, now. Drew's heart skipped at the mere sight of her, at the thought of what she had seen last night, and then at her dream, which had not been about her — and yet somehow, seeing Amber on that tiny, weathered boat brought with it the same familiarity that the woman in the dream had. And — hadn't she had the same birthmark, just on darker skin and around darker eyes?

When a man dressed in a long black trench coat and monocle barged past Drew, she realized she had been standing there for too long, staring at nothing at all, and shook her head before stepping onto the wooden planks of the docks. They creaked beneath her weight as though in warning — or perhaps encouragement.

"Morning." Drew attempted to keep her voice even as she said it. She rested against the bars the way the two of them had yesterday. It was a gray morning further inland, the river murky and stagnant[5] and not at all as comforting as it had felt on the pier.

Amber glanced up, face wrinkled in concentration as she collected her fishing gear and put it away. The boat rocked with her movements. Half-washed away and covered in barnacles, the title on the side named it *Diane*. "Morning. Isn't it a little bit early for a rock star to be up?"

"I think to qualify as a rock star you have to sell over at least ten CDs," Drew replied with a wry smile. "Catch anything?"

"Less than usual," she murmured, hauling her boxes onto shore. "But enough."

Drew could imagine her sitting on a boat that was almost as small as her, alone and at peace, eyes closed against the wind.... She would like to see her in action, wondered whether she was the same Amber out on the sea, or whether she let that veil of hostility fall away with the breeze.

"I'd like to try it sometime, if you'd have me," Drew said without thinking.

"You want to go fishing?" Amber frowned, putting her hands on her hips. She wore gray overalls that drowned her small frame, her thick thermal socks tucked into scuffed brown boots. Though Drew hadn't been able to picture her this way last night, she could see now that this was where she belonged — liked it, even: liked that she was unapologetically her, with her bare face and her dirty clothes. She was not trying to be anyone other than a fisherwoman in a small coastal town — not like Drew, with all of the eyeliner she put on before shows and the way she drummed to drown out the noise of her own mind wondering always where she would go next and who she would be.

"If you'd have me," Drew repeated with a shrug, hope clear in the question. She had always been this way: wanting to pick up new pieces of herself everywhere she went, new hobbies and new experiences. Perhaps one day it would help her to understand who she was and what she wanted.

"I'm going out again tomorrow afternoon," Amber said, her tone lacking any sort of commitment. Perhaps she doubted Drew's sincerity, or perhaps she couldn't think of anything worse than taking Drew out on her boat. "You're welcome to come, if you want."

"Tomorrow afternoon sounds perfect," Drew agreed, excitement sparking in her chest. "That reminds me — I didn't get to thank you last night for the ghost tour."

"Oh, please." Amber waved her off, tucking a loose strand of hair behind her ear before continuing her work. Drew would have helped her if she'd had any idea what Amber was even doing with the boat and the tackle boxes. She didn't, though, and didn't want to get under her feet with her cluelessness. "I know Ethan roped you into that."

"No." Drew shook her head. "I wanted to, and I enjoyed it. Thank you."

"Well, I got to hear your band play, so I suppose we're even." Only a ghost of a smile wavered on Amber's lips — but still, it was there, telling Drew that she should keep talking, keep trying. For what, she didn't know. "You're pretty good, by the way."

"Thank you. That's definitely an improvement from 'not bad.'" Drew hadn't been expecting the compliment, and didn't know what to do with it. "So... I was wondering if perhaps you'd like to do something when you're finished up here. The band are still asleep, and I don't really know my way around. Actually, I kind of wanted to get my tarot cards read over there. I've never done it before and it sounds interesting."

Drew was babbling. She knew it even when she pointed over to the line of striped tents. Her cheeks heated with embarrassment, and only burned further when Amber arched an eyebrow.

"I don't really believe in that stuff," Amber said. Drew could tell she had lost interest. She should have just shut up when Amber had agreed to the fishing trip. "I think Mabel has been ripping people off with that crystal ball of hers for longer than I've been alive."

"Ah." Drew nodded, trying to hide her disappointment. If she didn't believe in tarot cards, she certainly wouldn't want to hear about Drew's dreams. "I suppose I'll see you at the party tonight, then."

"You will." Another small smile. Another flicker of light in Drew's chest.

"Good."

Drew waved Amber off and trudged away from the docks before she could make any more of a fool of herself. The dream she had had this morning was long, long forgotten now

∞ ∞ ∞

Amber had been right about Mabel ripping off her visitors. Drew's purse was fifteen pounds lighter when she entered the medium's tent.

It was lit inside with fairy lights, and a crystal ball sat in the center of a small table, just as Amber had said. Behind it was Mabel, she assumed, an older woman with red hair that bled to gray at the roots and deep-crimson lipstick that sank into the wrinkles around her mouth. There were no amulets or long nails, no headscarves or fancy dresses, as Drew had been expecting. No, just a middle-aged woman sitting soberly beside a cloth-covered table.

"Welcome," Mabel greeted her, her voice soft as honey and her lips curling into a pleased grin. Her two front teeth were stained with lipstick. "You have come to seek something."

"For that price, I hope I find it." It was a joke, but if Mabel found it amusing, she did not show it, instead clasping her hands together and sighing.

"What will it be, then? Palm reading or tarot cards?"

Drew gestured to the glass ball as she sat down across from the woman. "What does that do?"

"Nothing," Mabel answered, swiping the ball away to the edge as though it were merely a distraction. "I use it for decoration."

Drew hid her smirk. It was a good job, really, that Amber wasn't here. God help poor Mabel if she had been. "Can you read both?"

"I can." She nodded, flexing her fingers as though to say *Come here*. Drew offered her hand, palm up. Her hands were calloused and blistered from drumming, and tender to the touch when Mabel traced a brittle fingernail across the lines etched in her flesh. "This is your dominant hand?"

Drew had not thought of it that way for so long — always using both hands when playing the drums or the piano and never using them for much else — that she had to think. "Yes."

"You're a musician," she pointed out sagely.

"Yes, I am."

"Good. The arts are where you are supposed to be."

Drew bit her lip to keep her retort suppressed. She knew that, had known it her whole life, and had not needed to pay to be told so.

"You have 'water hands.' You are well in tune with what goes on up here" — Mabel pressed her spare hand to the space between Drew's eyebrow — "and here." Her hand fell to her sternum before returning to Drew's fingers. "It means you see and feel things others don't. Perhaps you are more connected to the world around you. You understand more because your heart and mind remain open."

Drew's palms were beginning to grow clammy, her heart stuttering in her chest. She had never thought of it that way, but perhaps it was true. Perhaps that was the reason for her déjà vu and her strange dreams, the way she somehow felt connected to this town and the people — well, just one person — in it.

Mabel traced the top line of her palm, from index finger to the fleshy edge. "You are made to fall in love with only one person in your lifetime.

If you grow restless in future relationships, you might take it as a sign that you are with the wrong one."

"You mean like a soul mate?" Drew swallowed, words slipping out in no more than a whisper. She felt silly even saying such a word, but it came to her easily now. The watch felt heavier in her pocket than it had before, weighed down by the words and the dreams.

"A soul mate, a twin flame." Mabel shrugged. "Someone who is tethered to you in this life and perhaps others."

"Others?"

"Past lives," she elaborated. "Future lives. Who you were and who you may be."

"You believe that we can be other people?" Drew leaned forward in her chair, the pungent incense floating up from a wooden box beside the crystal ball near choking her. "With other lives?"

"I believe it." Mabel nodded. Her green eyes were vacant, as though she were no longer looking at Drew's palms but at something else entirely. "You should, too, for I can tell there are many stories in you. You have lived many lives, have wandered this earth for centuries to find them."

"Who?" Blood rushed to Drew's ears, her head, her hands, energy and fear pulsing through every inch of her. Thank god it was dark. Thank god her blush would not be so visible in the glow of the fairy lights.

"The one you are tethered to." Mabel said it

as though it was the simplest thing in the world. "Your twin flame. Your equal."

"But there can't be just one person I'm meant to find," Drew countered, snatching her hand away. She didn't want to hear any more. This had done her no good; it was only making her more paranoid, more confused... more naive and hopeful. "People aren't built for that. We fall in love again and again."

"Not always with the right people," Mabel replied, and dragged the crystal ball back to the center of the table. The reading was over, then. "I can sense your attachment without needing to read your palm, child. Your fate was sealed long ago. Perhaps you have already found them. Perhaps it will take lifetimes to. Perhaps you never will because you refuse to see it."

Drew shook her head and stood up, the chair rocking against the backs of her knees. "What you're saying means nothing. You're just here for the money, like everybody else. I didn't pay to solve riddles."

Mabel's devouring gaze turned cold as she crossed her arms over her chest. "Then why are you in my tent?"

Drew only realized that she had no answer when she opened her mouth and no words came. Why *was* she here? Why was she letting an old woman dictate who she was, who she was meant to be? It was rubbish, all of it. It was not as though Mabel could know for certain if past lives or soul mates existed. It was not as though she knew that Drew had been feeling strange. It was not as though she knew about the pocket watch hidden in her jacket.

"I changed my mind about the tarot," Drew said, gathering her purse up quickly. "Thanks for the reading."

"When you're ready, you may come back to claim the rest."

"I don't think so." Drew slid the curtain back, daylight blinding her, before Mabel could say any more. She was glad when chatter and fresh air and the smell of something cooking greeted her. Glad when she left the tent and did not dare look back.

Ten

Amber was up to her elbows in pumpkin innards. The kitchen table was covered in its flesh and seeds, the sweet smell overwhelming as she scraped out the last of the third one she had disemboweled today. The other two sat carved on the counter: one with pointed fangs and the other a goofy-looking thing that had not been meant to turn out so... mangled.

She had promised Ethan to bring a few for the party tonight, since he was busy helping out the town with their festivities all weekend. With her shirt covered in orange goo, though, and her hair matted with the vile stuff, she regretted her offer now.

"Can I help?" The voice was meek and uncertain, and one that she was not used to hearing around this house. Amber turned her head to peer over her shoulder and found Emily at the threshold, red hair damp from her shower and sweater sleeves pulled over her hands.

Amber would have snapped out a "no" if she were not so desperate to be done with the whole ordeal. "Are you any good?"

"Practically a pro," she joked with a dry

smile, bare feet padding onto the kitchen tiles cautiously. "My family and I used to carve them every year."

Amber motioned with her spoon to the set of drawers by the sink. "Knives and spoons are in there."

She did not bother to clear a space for her at the table, though perhaps she should have; instead she watched Emily pull the utensils out and set them down, sweeping away the two bowls of pumpkin pulp in her way before sitting. There were two pumpkins left to carve; Emily, thankfully, took the largest and began her work by selecting a marker.

"Is there any particular design you're going for?"

Amber shrugged. The one she was making now was an assortment of crescent moons and stars. "Anything you want. Ethan can make do with what he gets."

"It's for the party tonight, then?" Clearly, Emily was scrabbling for any conversation she could get. Amber would much rather work in silence, even if her question did cover up the sound of squelching her spoon made as she scooped.

"Yep," Amber answered. "Are you going?"

"Kit wants to." She smiled, eyes crinkling at the corners. "He said he'd let me do his face paint."

"Lucky you." Amber couldn't help the sarcasm that crept into her words as she scraped out the last of the pulp and sat down. Her back was aching, and blisters were beginning to form on her hands from the constant grip on the spoon and knives. Was this how Drew felt, always playing the drums?

Not that she was thinking about Drew, or Drew playing the drums.

"What are you going as?" The tip of Emily's tongue poked out as she concentrated on carving out the top of the pumpkin.

Amber sighed, already regretting her decision to let her help. Whatever had happened to good old-fashioned silence? "A scarecrow. You?"

"I'm not sure yet. Maybe you could help me."

"I'm sure Kit will," she said. "He used to help with my costume and face paint when we were younger."

Emily paused her sawing, cheeks dimpling as her smile deepened. "He's missed you a lot, you know."

Amber scowled, her grip on the knife slipping so that she almost lost a finger. Had this been Emily's plan? To play the role of loyal girlfriend and help get Kit back into Amber's good graces? "He could have fooled me."

"He has," she insisted. "He talks about you almost every day — about everything you did as kids. He loves you very much. You're lucky to have a brother like that."

Amber cut Emily an icy glare that put an end to her rambling. "It won't work."

"What won't?" Emily questioned innocently, picking up her knife again and finishing her removal of the stalk.

"Whatever it is you're trying to do."

"I just —" She hesitated, biting down on her bottom lip and giving Amber a pitiful look that made her skin crawl. "I see how much not talking to you hurts him. How much *you* hurt him. I hope I'm not the reason for it — I mean, I hope I haven't come between the two of you."

"It's not about you," Amber mumbled, fighting against the guilt threatening to swallow her.

"Good." Emily nodded.

Silence fell over them — a welcome one, as far as Amber was concerned. She had carved out half of the moons and stars on her pumpkin when Emily finally spoke again.

"I lost my sister a few years ago." Her voice shook with tears that Amber prayed would not fall: that was the last thing she wanted to deal with. Still, the revelation unsettled her stomach enough that she faltered, looking up from her pumpkin. Emily's green eyes were dry, but her chin wobbled ever so slightly. "You don't realize how much you take them for granted until they're gone."

"I don't see what that has to do with Kit and me," Amber responded quietly.

"Kit isn't gone yet, Amber. But he will be, eventually — whether that's because you push him away completely or, heaven forbid, because of some other reason. Either way, you're making a mistake. He tries so hard with you, even when he shouldn't have to. You'll regret taking that for granted one day."

"I don't need you to tell me what it means to lose someone." Amber's eyes flashed to the portrait of her mother hanging on the wall behind Emily for only a moment, and yet it was enough to clog her throat with that familiar, sharp lump.

"I know that," Emily answered, "and I'm sorry for it. But Kit is your brother, and he loves you, whether he's here or in Edinburgh or somewhere else entirely. It would be a shame if you didn't realize just how precious that is."

Amber's jaw clenched in anger, grief and regret and frustration roiling through her with burning-hot claws. "Either way, it makes no difference to you, does it?"

Emily blinked, unfazed by the dig. "It does if you keep hurting him" was all she said before continuing her work on the pumpkin.

Amber wished she had another retort, but she didn't have the energy to so much as scoff. Instead she gulped down her rising tears and sawed through the pumpkin with a new aggressiveness.

It wasn't the prying or the accusations that filled Amber with so much ire. No, it was the fact that deep down, she knew Emily was right.

How much longer could she stand to hate her brother?

Eleven

Ethan's farm was almost unrecognizable once he and the band were finished with it. Gravestones planted in the soil made the front yard look just as the church had on the ghost walk the night before, and Amber had brought enough pumpkins with her that the tail end of her father's car had been weighed down with them.

Drew and the rest of the band had spent the entire day decorating it inside and out with skeletons, hay bales, rubber spiders, and fake blood. It was only when the eerie green lights from inside began to glow and the music began to play that Drew began to feel out of place without a costume. She had let Max paint her face with an excessive amount of black eyeshadow and a little red dribble down her chin that resembled blood, but other than that, she did not fit in at all with the people beginning to linger by the camper in Ethan's front yard.

She certainly did not fit in with Amber. Drew did a double take when she emerged from the house wearing a straw hat, her face painted with browns and blacks and oranges to make her look like a scarecrow. Her brown overalls, which

Drew had thought were her everyday attire earlier, were now stuffed with hay, her blonde hair barely reaching her shoulders in two plaits. Drew might not have recognized her at all if it weren't for those piercing blue eyes — near translucent in the twilight — and her small frame.

"You went all out," Drew observed as she approached. The painted corners of her mouth were downturned as though the party was her idea of a nightmare.

"I was forced against my will," Amber huffed, leaning against the camper.

"Ethan?"

"Ethan," she confirmed, removing her hat and scratching her hairline. "This thing is itchy."

Drew would have laughed, would have acknowledged how much she wanted to reach out and soothe her irritation, if it weren't for something locking her in place and turning her cold.

An image: a flash of one that lasted only a second of a man lifting his top hat to her — the same man she had seen in her dream last night emerging from the coach with a woman, the man she had almost forgotten entirely. The sight of him had awakened her again now, though, freezing her to the spot as Amber tucked her hat under her arm and ruffled her hair, oblivious.

"Why hasn't he roped you into dressing up, anyway?" She nodded to Drew's clothes. They were not much different than what she usually wore for gigs, though she had swapped her jeans for fishnet tights and a short skirt that showed off all of the lumps and bumps she hated around her thighs.

"He'll have to catch me first," she said, voice still dazed and distant as déjà vu lurched her stomach forward — toward Amber. She sucked in a breath, forced herself to look away.

Mist lingered down the hill, party guests emerging from the gray as they made their way up. Drew hadn't realized before how high up they were. Now she used that to distract herself, tried to find buildings that she recognized jutting among the cliffs.

"Besides, I'm dressing up as someone who doesn't care about Halloween."

"Why not?"

Drew shrugged, putting her hands in her pockets to disguise their trembling. They grazed the watch — that damn watch that she had spent too much money on, and that now seemed to haunt her day and night. How much longer could she do this? Endure this without understanding what it was? She thought of Mabel, of what she had said and the things she had seemed to know without Drew telling her. Could any of it be true?

She'd almost forgotten Amber's question and licked her plum-painted lips despite the fact that Max would scold her for wiping away the dark color. "It never really lives up to expectations, does it? I feel like I'm always waiting for something more... exciting."

Amber tilted her head as though pondering the answer. "Well, try making the effort and you never know what might come of it." In one swift movement, Amber reached out and swiped a pointed hat from a passing witch who was already stumbling around with a beer in her hand. "Here."

She placed the hat on Drew's head with a small smile that made her smile, too. "Suits you."

"Oi!" the witch shouted, but staggered down the pumpkin-lined path without demanding the hat be returned. Drew couldn't help but laugh in surprise — for Amber more than the stranger. As though reading it on her face, Amber shrugged.

"If I have to do it" — she waved her straw hat around — "so do you."

"I suppose it's only fair," Drew agreed, readjusting the hat and the dark curtain of curls on her shoulders.

Amber's eyes turned stony as she averted them to the gate. Drew followed her gaze, glimpsing a man and woman she didn't recognize casting her a quick wave. Whoever it was, it was clear that Amber didn't want to see them. Still, she murmured an "Excuse me," and left Drew feeling hollow in her absence.

Drew had a feeling that it was not the first time she had watched Amber walk away. Likelier still was that it would not be the last.

The conversation she was caught in did not seem pleasant. Amber crossed her arms over her chest, expression twisted with cruelty as she spat something to the couple.

"You sure like 'em mean, don't you?" Rusty's husky voice in Drew's ear caused her to start, cheeks heating even as the cold bit into them.

"What are you talking about?"

Rusty motioned to where Amber stood with a nod, a smug grin on her lips. She, too, had not bothered to dress up — and god help Ethan if he so much as asked. "Miss This Is *My* Private Driveway over there." She mimicked Amber's Yorkshire accent as she said it, sucking in her cheeks and fluttering her eyelashes. "You're obsessed."

"I'm not obsessed." Drew rolled her eyes, though she sounded unconvincing even to herself. "And she's not so bad once you get to know her."

"If you say so." Rusty shot her a withering look and winced when she heard Ethan's voice floating over the din of the guests gathering across the grass. "That's my cue to go wherever he isn't."

Drew shook her head, relief drawing her breath from her. She didn't want to talk about Amber with Rusty — or with anyone else, for that matter. Not until she figured out what was happening in her own head. Not until she understood why sometimes Amber summoned images, memories, of other people from other lives that Drew had not recalled living until now. Worse was that Amber seemed not to even realize it.

"Drew Dawson!" Ethan shouted from the veranda, cupping a hand to his mouth and flinching when he caught his face on the scissor gloves his hands bore. He had gone all out as Edward Scissorhands, fake scars peppered everywhere and all, and his hair curled and backcombed in a mass of black atop his head. His ghastly white face floated, disembodied, in the shadows. "Come and dance with me!"

Drew tried to ignore the attention drawn to her as she made her way up the path — and tried to ignore the pull that left her wanting to look back to Amber before she disappeared into the chaos of the party.

Twelve

"Well, this is definitely far better than anything I ever forced you to wear for Halloween growing up," Kit praised, admiring Amber's costume. Ethan had forced her to sit on his bed for an hour as he applied her makeup, copying a tutorial on You-Tube, and she could admit that it had paid off — even if the straw hat was causing her more discomfort than anything else she might have worn.

She only placed her hands in the front pocket of her dungarees, hay stolen straight from the stables rustling in her sleeves. "Ethan's doing."

"I might have guessed." His eyes glinted as he looked up at the house. He and Emily were matching — a fact that made her nauseated — vampires, with plastic fangs that he pulled out of his mouth now along with a string of saliva. "Emily told me she helped with the pumpkins."

Amber glanced at Emily. If she was expecting a thanks for inviting herself to carve pumpkins as an excuse to pry into her business with her brother, she wasn't going to get it. "She did."

Kit shifted awkwardly. "We were thinking of staying for the rest of the week, if it's okay by you. That way we can enjoy bonfire night, too."

"It's not up to me." Amber shrugged. "It's no skin off my back either way."

"Nose," he corrected. "It's 'no skin off my nose.'"

Amber pursed her lips into a thin line. "Either way, I don't care."

Kit turned to Emily, itching the lobe of his ear. As though it was some sort of code, she nodded and unlinked her arm from his. "I'm going to go and get us some drinks, I think."

Amber's glare followed her long after she had passed them, and only then did she look her brother in the eye again.

"You know, Emily is really trying with you."

"Oh, I know." The bitterness tasted foul in her mouth, but she couldn't swallow it down — could only spit it out, like something rotten. "We had a lovely bonding experience earlier."

"It doesn't have to be like this all the time." Kit sighed in exasperation. "Aren't you tired of it?"

Yes, she wanted to say. *Yes, I'm tired of it.* Instead she scowled silently beneath her hat. Around them, the guests were oblivious to the argument, slurred words and singing floating around them but never touching them.

At Amber's silence, Kit only scoffed and shook his head. He had left his hair curly tonight so that he looked more like his old self: the self that Amber had grown up with. It didn't change the fact that he had left her alone.

"You know, Mum would be so disappointed

in us. She raised us to care for each other, even when we were bickering constantly. But this isn't bickering, Amber, is it?"

He knew what the words did to her — knew they would be a punch to her gut — and yet he had said them anyway. She hated him for that, hated him for all of it. Her nostrils flared, throat burning. "Don't use her as a way to get to me, Kit," she warned, voice low.

"I'm not using her. It's the truth."

Amber looked away, shivering in the cold. Her heart thrummed painfully in her chest, body tingling with emotions she could still not confront, even now.

"I keep trying, but it's not worth it, is it?" Kit questioned, voice cracking. "You're too damn stubborn to ever forgive me, to ever see things from my side."

"Do you see things from my side?" Her voice rose, thick with the promise of tears she could no longer control. God, she was tired. "You left me *alone*, Kit. You left *us* alone."

He frowned. "You have Dad."

"Dad is Dad," she shot back. "He isn't you. He —" The words broke on her lips, and she swallowed, wiping the tears from her cheeks quickly. The dampness bit at her flesh against the cold. "I know that I'm supposed to be an adult. I know that I'm supposed to tell you to go and be happy because you deserve to be. But I just can't."

"Why?" Kit asked gently. He made no attempt to comfort her, to reach out, but that was probably because he knew if he did, Amber would pull away. He knew her too well — and yet not at all. Not anymore.

"Because Mum died and you just… left," she whispered. "Months after, you just left. Knowing we were struggling with the business and with losing her. You left me alone, Kit. You moved on."

"I didn't move on." His face softened, and he took a step closer to her. "I'm still here, Amber. I always will be."

She shook her head, feeling as fragile as a child. She dreaded to think of how she must look: her face paint was probably streaked with her tears.

"It's not the same." She took a jagged breath, finding the courage to look up at him, to say the words she had been longing to for months, years. "I lost my mother and my brother in the space of a few months, Kit. I'm glad you found your happiness, but I didn't find mine. I still haven't — so I'm sorry if I make it difficult. I'm sorry if I'm rude to your girlfriend. But I can't look at you without feeling…"

She couldn't finish that sentence, even now.

"Amber," he breathed, placing a hand on her arm finally. She let him, if only for the warmth, and because she was drained now that she had finally gotten it off her chest. "I'm your brother. I will always be your brother. Just because things aren't the same doesn't mean *we* aren't the same.

But pushing me away won't bring me back."

She closed her eyes, inhaling the sharp freshness of the night with an aching chest and an aching soul. "I know" was all she could find it in her to say.

"So can this be the end of it?" Hope swelled in the question. "Can we go back to arguing over who ate the last custard cream?"

"I'll try," she said, all that she could promise him. It seemed to be enough, for he nodded and gathered her into a hug. She let him, though it all still swirled inside her like paint, turning her stomach into murky shades of brown and gray.

Still, he was right: her mother wouldn't have wanted this for them.

For her, she would at least try to let it all go.

Thirteen

She can feel the red devil horns sitting atop her head as she watches him play. His back is heavy with white-feathered wings, hanging down over the piano stool. The angel and the devil.

Her eyes, near black in the light of the club, glitter as though she can feel what he feels in the melody singing out from his light taps on the ivory keys. Nobody else cares. Nobody else stops to watch. Only her. Good. Hers is the only attention he cares about, anyway.

She sucks down on her crimson lip as the tempo fades out slowly, leaning across the shining black piano onto her elbows. He can see her in the reflection, a silhouette with two pointed protrusions sticking out of her hair. It makes him lose control of his tune, makes him pause before he plays the end note in a wavering finale. Her gaze burns him with a fire belonging to hell itself, and he wonders if perhaps this is not a costume — if perhaps she truly is the devil incarnate. Everything about her screams infernally with it, from the way her hips sway to the way she blinks to reveal red-painted eyelids glittering beneath the chandelier.

It is almost unbearable, to sit so close to her.

And yet he cannot move away. She has him ensnared here, on this stool, and she knows it. He reaches out a trembling hand, lets the pad of his thumb graze the birthmark-stained cheek.

She pulls it away and kisses his fingertips delicately. "Anyone would think we planned for this."

It takes him a moment to realize that she means the costumes. "I don't feel so angelic anymore."

Her cheeks dimple when she grins, white teeth flashing as she moves around the piano to sit beside him. When her elbow brushes his ribcage, he shivers.

"Here," she murmurs, pulling the horns off her head and slipping them onto his own, despite the soft curls that live there. Then she pulls out the pocket watch and checks the time it has been frozen at since the moment they met. Ten thirty. "How's that?"

His breath catches, eyes flitting down to her curling lips.

"Much better."

∞ ∞ ∞

"What do you think?" The vision swimming before her melded into one of Max, adjusting her pointed red horns atop her pink hair. "Ethan found them for me."

Drew still felt as though she were dreaming, even as the soft piano melody was swapped for the *Ghostbusters* theme tune and she realized that she was not sitting but standing.

"They're nice" was all she could force out. "I'll be back in a minute."

Drew snatched a tangle of fake cobwebs from her face as she left the house through the kitchen. Hours of being deafened by the same dozen Halloween songs had taken its toll, and even with a concoction of spirits that Ethan had poured for her in her hand, she was no longer interested in dancing. Perhaps that made her miserable; perhaps she didn't care.

The backyard was significantly quieter than the front, with only a few smokers loitering by the kitchen door. The stables were barely visible in the fog that had thickened through the night, though she could hear the sound of the horses whickering not too far away — and then a gentle voice soothing them.

Drew abandoned her drink and trod on unsteady feet until a golden glow broke the blanket of fog. The stables were empty save for her, for Amber. Drew pushed down the feelings and images threatening to resurface again at the sight of her stroking the horse's chestnut mane, pretending that she did not see that brown-haired, brown-skinned girl in the way that she smiled softly and muttered in the horse's ear with all the care she never seemed to show anyone else. Instead, Drew made herself known by kicking up a stray bit of hay on the floor.

Amber started, and then her shoulders sagged when she realized that it was only Drew.

Her face paint had become patchy and smudged, and her straw hat was long gone. Still, the birthmark around her eye was mostly covered, and Drew was relieved. Perhaps for a few moments she could pretend it was not there, pretend that Amber was not haunting her every waking moment here in different faces and different places — always with that telltale mark.

"I always seem to find you standing alone."

"I'm not alone," Amber replied, gaze remaining steady on the horse. "I have Stoker."

"Hanging out with a horse at a party?" A small smile twitched on Drew's lips as she reached them, her hand brushing the horse's muzzle gently. She had never been around horses before — not in this life, anyway.

Heavens above, she was beginning to sound like Mabel — yet she couldn't think of another explanation for the visions, the déjà vu, the feelings arising even now when she stood beside her. A tether, Mabel had said. A part of her did feel tethered by the very pits of her stomach, and that tether tugged and tugged for her to take another step, to get closer.

"Well, we go way back. Old friends, aren't we, Stoker?" Amber laughed softly, but there was something sad that made it stick in her throat all wrong. Stoker grunted at the same time that Drew frowned.

"Everything okay?"

Amber shrugged noncommittally, face half

hidden behind Stoker's muzzle so that Drew couldn't quite see her expression.

"Anything to do with the couple you were talking to earlier?" She shouldn't be prying, and yet she couldn't help herself — wanted to know everything and anything about her. Even the sight of her out here alone, knowing that something was wrong, left a burning ache in Drew's chest, as though Amber's pain was also hers. It was difficult to remember that Drew had not even known her until yesterday.

"My brother and his girlfriend," Amber explained with a solemn sigh.

"You don't get on?" The warmth of Stoker's coat as she buried her fingers into his mane was a comfort, the fresh, sharp smell of hay taking her somewhere other than here, where people weren't drinking themselves silly and stained with fake blood, to an open space — to the space she had dreamed of last night.

"It's complicated," Amber said, voice thickening. Drew could not tell if it was from sadness or evasion. Either way, as Amber gazed wistfully past her to the house, Drew saw what churned in those brilliant walls of ice.

"You're lonely," Drew observed, no hint of a question there.

Amber blinked, surprise flickering across her features for only a moment before she hid it away again. "Isn't everyone?"

"You don't have to be," Drew whispered, unsure even as she said it what she meant by it, what she was suggesting. Still, it felt right to say.

Amber worried at her lip, nothing like the devil-horned woman from the image she had glimpsed… and yet, at the same time, everything like her: in the way her eyes shone and the way she tucked her hair behind her ear; in the way she made Drew feel.

"Maybe not," Amber finally said. "Can I show you something?"

The way she lit up with the question had Drew wanting nothing more, so she nodded eagerly, feeling childish as her heart sped up. Amber bid Stoker a good night with a gentle pat before leading Drew out of the far end of the stables, and into the eerie gray beyond.

Fourteen

It had been years since Amber had last been any-where near the tree house. Ethan's father had built it when they were just children, and they had spent the better part of their youth in the confines of the wooden, slatted walls.

It appeared slowly out of the fog now, so far away from the house that they could barely hear the music still playing within. The flashing of strobe lights in the windows was the only evidence that they had not strayed too far. Amber felt silly even bringing Drew here, and yet it had felt right in the stables. Seeing her always seemed to awaken a nostalgia in her, a longing.

Amber climbed the ladder first, feeling Drew's eyes burning into her back as she let out a small, breathy laugh behind her. "I thought people only had tree houses in movies."

"Ethan begged and begged for this thing," she replied, voice strained from the effort it took to pull herself up onto the platform. When she turned, Drew was already on her way up too, her skirt riding up her thighs. Amber blushed and looked away, taking a big gulp of the brisk air to soothe the anguish she had felt all night. It was easy to pretend that none of that existed now, with the ground no longer visible beneath the curling mist and everything else wrapped in shadows. She wondered if her brother was still at the party, and then let the thought dissolve along with her surroundings.

Drew was breathless by the time she made it up the ladders, shimmying her leather skirt back down without any hint of embarrassment. Amber liked that about her: she was never anything but herself, never hid how she felt or what she wanted to say.

"I hope it's easier to get down," she joked, the old wood creaking as she gripped the railings.

Amber smiled and sat down, letting her feet dangle over the edge. She had forgotten just how weightless being up here made her feel, and was surprised that she could feel that way even now, as an adult, without all of the naivety and playfulness.

"I used to hide up here without even Ethan knowing sometimes," she said as Drew sat beside her. She was a warm presence on a cold night, and no longer an unwelcome one. "I'd pretend it was my home and that I'd never have to come down."

"I can see why." Drew leaned back on her hands, kicking her legs out like a child. "It's…" She paused, searching for the right word. "Peaceful."

Amber nodded and freed her hair of their braids, leaving the ties around her wrist as she shook out the kinks. She wished she could wipe off the paint that was now cracking and drying on her face.

"Thank you for bringing me up here." Drew's gravelly voice was so soft that Amber looked at her in surprise. She was all soft curves and darkness in the night's shadows, her eyes a warmer shade of black than the sky behind her and her lips a deep, faded purple.

"You know, you're familiar to me, too." Perhaps it was the way Drew looked that dragged it out of her, or perhaps it was the gentle tug in Amber's chest, or perhaps it was the fact that Drew kept seeming to catch her at her worst and yet never balked, but Amber couldn't keep herself from admitting it a moment longer. "You don't feel like a stranger."

Drew swallowed, tucking her hair behind her ear. Her witch's hat was long gone, now, but she didn't need it. She was already dark and seductive — spellbinding, even.

"I feel like I'm going mad," Drew whispered. "I see you everywhere I go, in everything I do, and I don't know why."

Amber furrowed her eyebrows in confusion. "What do you mean?"

Cheeks glowing red, Drew laughed and shook her head. "Nothing. Ignore me. I've had one too many to drink."

It was true that Amber could smell the alcohol on her breath, could see the light sheen of sweat coating her forehead and causing tendrils of hair to stick to her skin. She didn't seem all that drunk, though; she had managed climbing the ladder without a stumble.

Still, Amber accepted the excuse with only a bit of hesitation, sighing and lifting her head to bathe in the moon's light. She shivered once against the cold, and then Drew was there, settling her jacket across Amber's shoulders. The smell of must lingered on it, mixed with a rich, heady perfume that fit Drew perfectly.

Amber smiled appreciatively and pulled it tighter around herself, if only to bask in the parts of her that clung to the old leather. "Thank you."

A howl rent the night before Drew could reply, and her eyes widened into saucers. "Is that the beast again?"

The sheer ludicrousness caused an unexpected laugh to burble deep within Amber's throat, and with it, Drew laughed too. "Do you believe in all that stuff?"

Drew shrugged, something grave seeping through the cracks of her facade. "I don't know what I believe anymore." She lay back, gazing at the stars absently. "You were right about Mabel the medium, though. Absolute rip-off."

Amber scoffed. "What did she have to say for herself?"

"Nothing that made any sense." A strand of hair rested over Drew's face, and Amber resisted the urge to brush it away with her fingers. They tingled, though, begging to reach out and touch her, if only for a moment. Amber had never seen anybody as beautiful as her, with her round cheeks and dark skin, all delicate and subtle features on a person that was anything but.

"That sounds like Mabel," Amber mumbled with an amused tut, sighing when the breeze ripped through her hair and soothed her scalp, aching after the tightness of the braids. Free. She was free. The only other time she'd felt this way was on her boat, when she was alone — always alone. Now she was anything but.

She let herself lie down beside Drew, feet still dangling over the edge of the platform. Crunching leaves greeted her, clinging to her hair and rustling in her ear. Drew turned her face to her, and as though it had been an invitation, her ringed fingers twirled through Amber's roughly cut hair absently.

"I cut it myself," Amber explained self-consciously, though she didn't want to pull away now. Her mother used to play with her hair when she was younger, when it was longer and not quite so bleached by Whitby summers spent on the water. "The sea was always tangling it and drying it out, so I wanted it gone."

"I like it this way," Drew murmured.

Amber relaxed at the approval and turned her attention back to the sky. Two stars guttered between the clouds: one for Amber and one for Drew. God, she had missed it up here. It felt better now, lying beside Drew, than it ever had as a child.

"We should get back to the party," she said after a few moments.

"Yes," Drew agreed. "We should."

Instead of moving away, though, Drew shuffled closer, until their arms were pressing together and their warmth, breaths — visible in the night — mingled into one. They did not come down until hours later, when it was too cold to remain.

Even then, Amber wished she'd had more time.

Fifteen

It is easier to steal from the rich at a masquerade ball. He doesn't take all at once — no, he would get caught doing it that way. Instead he snatches the odd pearl bracelet or diamond brooch, grazes the coin purses when they are left abandoned in the cloakroom — a predator that nibbles rather than gorges.

He has never been caught before, until now. One moment his dainty, swift hands are in the pocket of a jacket still being worn, and the next, fingers are clenching his wrist. It is the man in the wolf mask, the one he saw outside earlier disembarking from the carriage.

All he can make out of him are his eyes, near translucent in the golden, guttering light of the chandeliers swinging overhead. They are ablaze — not with anger, but with an amusement that says, I've been waiting for you. His mouth says the same, curved into a soft, lopsided smirk.

The thief can do nothing, say nothing. This is foreign territory. He might be thrown out or reported. He might be incarcerated. Worse, even.

The aristocrat does not hint as to where his fate lies, instead pulling him through the twirling bodies and taffeta skirts and into the cloakroom. The *thief could try to fight it, try to run, but the man's grip is iron despite his lack of fury, and he does not fancy his chances. He will see how this plays out, first. Wait for the right moment to make a run for it.*

"I have been watching you all night," he says in a lilting French accent, peeling his mask off to reveal what lies underneath. The thief's breath catches in his throat. His face is heart-shaped, narrow, skin golden and blemished with a birthmark on the right side of his face. The thief is sure he has seen that birthmark before. "Your pockets must be full to the brim."

"Not full enough," he answers, as nonchalantly as he can, though he is certain he knows the man, has met him before somewhere else. Where? *And if he has been watching him, why hasn't he said anything until now?*

"Then take what you wish." The golden-haired, sharp-nosed man roots in his pockets and pulls out an old pocket watch etched with a faint date and a name. Augustin. 1717. *The thief had stumbled into this party after hearing about it by chance, but he knows that name: knows it because this very building, this very ballroom, and this very ball belongs to Claude Augustin. The same Claude Augustin, he wagers, who stands in front of him now.*

Augustin rifles further without noticing the thief's newfound, foreign fear, pulling out a jewelry box and a coin purse. "You are welcome to whatever else lies in this cloakroom, if you have not already bled it dry."

"What game is this?" the thief questions,

frowning, though the mask he had stolen earlier conceals it.

"No game." Augustin sniffs, as though he is allergic to his own wealth. "If you wish for material goods so badly that you came here tonight, you may take them."

When the thief makes no move to do so, Augustin grips his hand again, letting the pocket watch fall into his palm. It is heavy and cool even with his white gloves on. So valuable that anything else weighing down his hidden pockets means next to nothing in comparison.

"Take it," Augustin repeats. "I have no use for it. Neither do the rest of them. They all have more money out there than they know what to do with."

The thief tilts his head, eyes narrowed. "A trick."

"No," Augustin assures him, nodding to the lines of coats — all of which the thief rummaged through earlier to find the heaviest pockets, the purses with the most jingling.

He blinks, hesitating. He should not trust Augustin's word, and yet he has been watching him tonight after being so taken by him outside, has seen all of the ways he falters: his upright posture sags when nobody is looking; his smile falls when he turns his head away. Perhaps it is true. Perhaps money does not make the young man happy.

It certainly makes the thief happy, though. He approaches the coats cautiously, waiting for the catch. There is none, not even when he is stuffing his pockets with all sorts of jewelry and gemstones, when he has taken whole purses until he cannot possibly fit anything more on his person.

Augustin only watches him with those glittering, translucent eyes — curious eyes. Solemn eyes. Familiar eyes.

"Take your mask off," he orders when the thief is done.

There it is. "So you can have them sketch out my face and put it on every poster, every newspaper, in Paris?"

"So I might see who you are just once before you run off and do not come back."

The thief is not a fool. He doesn't move to untie the mask, doesn't move at all. Augustin takes a step toward him, and when the thief does not balk, he takes another, reaching his hands out. The thief can smell the sweet champagne on his breath, can feel it hitting his cheek. His wealth reeks from his very skin, a pungent scent of citrus and spice.

He swallows, eyes fluttering shut when delicate fingers find the ties hidden in his thick, dark hair. His heart is hammering in his chest, not because he is afraid of Paris's wealthiest man, but because he knows there will be no going back, no hiding from those eyes once it is off.

He is right. The air hits the exposed skin, the bridge of his nose, like a steel dagger — and yet his gaze is the blade that pierces and draws blood. The thief wants to snatch back his mask, but he curls his hands into fists in restraint. He won't give him the satisfaction, won't shrink from him no matter how much he wants to.

Augustin does not laugh or sneer, though. He only smiles as though he has never seen anything like him before.

The thief cannot do the same. He is too certain that he has seen Augustin's smile before, on another's lips.

∞ ∞ ∞

Drew hadn't meant to return to Mabel's tent. She had been wandering off the second strange dream she'd had in a row, mind racing with all of the reasons none of this made any sense at all, and had just happened across it. Perhaps it was all in her head, or perhaps she was going mad — but nobody else could help her.

Mabel was not inside. Instead she was folding up a sign by the curtain, the tent already half collapsed behind her. The rest of the bazaar was packing up too, the festival coming to an end as everyone returned to their normal lives. Would Drew be able to do the same?

It didn't feel that way.

Mabel's head snapped up as Drew came to a stop in front of her, still shifting from foot to foot undecidedly. Yet Mabel's green eyes locked her in place, and Drew knew she needed to stay.

"You're too late," she said coldly before

tucking the sign under her arm, her silk robes whispering across the cobblestones as she moved. She wore none of the heavy makeup she had yesterday, and she looked the older for it — the wiser, too. Her red hair was swept back from her shoulders in thick, wiry tresses. Were it not for her clothes, she might have looked completely normal. "We're closed."

"I was hoping you might make an exception," Drew replied, worrying at her lip. "We never did finish my reading."

"No, we didn't — and while I offered for you to return, I recall that you did not believe in my sight."

"Maybe I was wrong," Drew muttered quietly, eyes flitting around the bazaar as though afraid anyone else might hear her. Her bandmates were still hungover at Ethan's, though, and she was not meeting Amber until this afternoon. She had already attempted to look for the woman who had sold the pocket watch to her, but the stall was gone and Drew had a feeling the seller would not have been willing to help even if she had been there.

Mabel sighed, her lined face softening in defeat.

"Do you know anything about dreams?" Drew continued.

"What sort of dreams?" The way she asked it implied that she already knew the answer and was simply humoring Drew after the scene yesterday.

Drew shrugged, squinting though the day was overcast. She hadn't slept well, having left Amber at Ethan's late last night and then being awakened by the dream not much later. Her eyes ached with the tiredness, and she badly needed a shower to wash away the grime of the last two days — grime and other things that clung to her and made her feel as though she were no longer herself. "Dreams about other people in other times."

Mabel's long nails tugged at her earlobe, her lips pursing almost sympathetically. "Dreams are part of our subconscious. They sometimes reflect feelings we are too afraid to feel."

Drew already knew that, and waved the words away. "But the people in them. What about them?"

"Do you know them?"

It was a simple question, and yet Drew couldn't answer it. "I don't know. They share similarities with... other people I know, but I don't think I've met them directly."

Mabel's eyes narrowed, and she put the sign down, balancing it against a tall pole holding the bazaar's gazebo up. "What sort of similarities?"

"I don't know." Drew shrugged. Her cheeks were burning: she felt stupid again — ridiculous, even. "Birthmarks. Eyes. Smiles."

"And they are from the past?"

"Yes." She couldn't bear to say the word any

louder than in a whisper. Still, it was clear that Mabel heard, and she took a step toward Drew with an intent gaze that gripped her to the spot and made her want to squirm away.

"In all of them, you feel a connection with the other person?"

Drew felt as though she were being examined in a doctor's office. She could do nothing but answer with complete honesty, an honesty she had not allowed herself to have until now. "I'm not even sure it's me in the dreams. I'm always different. So are they. But yes, there's a connection."

"Our past lives are not always people that we recognize." Mabel nodded as though she were merely talking about the weather, and not reincarnation. "What triggered these dreams? How long ago did they start?"

"Just the other night." Drew swallowed. Her throat felt like sandpaper as she rooted for the pocket watch and held it up to the light. "When I came here. I bought this at the market, and not long after I met someone who felt... familiar, I suppose. In every vision, in every dream, this is here. How can that be?"

Mabel took the watch and examined it. "Objects sometimes serve as the cord connecting us to the past. It seems you have met your twin flame, and this watch serves to remind you of that. It is the same person you dream of; just as you are different in every lifetime, so are they. Your mind is telling you that as best it can, using the only resources it has. It is up to you whether you listen."

"But how do I know what's real?" she questioned desperately.

Mabel shrugged with a bony shoulder. "If you feel it, dear, it is real. Trust yourself."

Drew raked her hair back from her face, teeth chattering though she was not cold. None of it made sense. None of it. Mabel returned the watch and began to gather her things again, and Drew helped her by taking the sign. Her fingers trembled as she did. "What if the other person doesn't feel the same?"

"If they are who you think, they will," Mabel answered. "The trouble with these things is that you don't always recognize one another at the same time. It may take a while longer for them, or perhaps they already have a feeling. Either way, the universe has worked hard to bring the two of you together again. You must trust that it knows what it is doing."

Drew fought the urge to scoff as she followed Mabel through the bazaar with the sign. The universe had never done a thing for Drew in her life. God only knew what it had in store.

"In the meantime," Mabel continued, "perhaps you can remind them. Show them the watch. Take them to the places you dream of, or similar ones. If your memory can be triggered by these things, so might theirs be, too."

Drew's eyes narrowed, calculating. Perhaps she was not wholly convinced, but that didn't mean she was not willing to try.

The problem was that she had been fighting it. What would happen if she succumbed?

What would happen if Amber remembered, too?

Sixteen

It was strange to have somebody on her boat who wasn't her father. Strange, but not unwelcome.

Drew was barer than Amber had ever seen her, with her thick dark hair piled into a bun on top of her head and her face free of any makeup. Amber suspected that she had borrowed one of Ethan's coats to wear over her thick sweater and leggings, because it drowned her, made her look younger. She was beautiful, and more beautiful out on the water, a dark contrast against the pale gray sky and dull sea.

Perhaps Amber shouldn't be thinking of her that way, though.

Drew was more reserved than usual, her dark eyes staring distantly to the horizon as she stood beside Amber. Then again, it had been a late night last night. Perhaps she was just tired. Amber tried to convince herself of that as the silence gnawed away at her gut.

"So," she started in an attempt to break it, "what do you think of *Diane*?"

"Nice." Drew's smile was barely more than a twitch at the corner of her lips. "I do recall you judging us for naming our campervan, though."

"Boats are supposed to be named," Amber argued, squinting to gauge the next wave. It was a rougher day at sea than it had been in a while, the wind a passing visitor that rapped on the frail windows too heavily for her liking. Still, she'd been out in worse. "But I suppose you have a point."

"So why *Diane*?"

Amber bit down on her cheek to distract herself from the lump that gathered in her throat every time the question was asked — which was rare these days, since the locals knew everything about everyone and thus knew better than to bring the name up to Amber or her father.

"Diane was the name of my mother." Her voice was little more than a faint mumble, and she stopped the motor to gather her tackle. The boat rocked beneath her feet, sliding over the waves and causing her to sway. Amber's home, her passion, was much more unstable than most.

"Oh." Drew inhaled softly in understanding. "I'm sorry."

Amber only shrugged and busied her hands by assembling the rods.

"Did she fish too?"

Amber nodded. "She taught me most of what I know. My dad taught me the rest."

"She'd be proud of you, then."

Amber scoffed, remembering Kit's words from last night. "I'm not so sure about that."

"Amber..." Drew whispered, and just the way she said her name had Amber on the verge of tears. She swallowed them down, locked them away deep in her stomach. She wouldn't do this today. She barely knew Drew — a fact she had to keep reminding herself of, especially after last night.

Even as she looked anywhere but at Drew, her hands found Amber's and squeezed. They were clammy and full of calluses, but that did not make her touch any less of a comfort. A comfort, and a risk. A risk that Amber was not willing to take now. She pulled her hand away and tried to ignore the look of hurt that flashed across Drew's face.

"Shall we go fishing, or shall we sit and cry about our tragic pasts all day?" The question was rhetorical; Amber thrust a line into Drew's hand before she could choose the latter option and guided her out of the cabin. The wind bit into her cheeks, as confronting as a wall of ice in comparison to the peace she had felt inside, but she did not turn around.

She did not want to face Drew, or the boat, or the reminders of her mother in everything she did. She only wanted to fish, and so she did.

Seventeen

Drew had not caught a thing: not even an old boot, or a small mackerel. She followed Amber with the fishing pole as closely as she could, and yet nothing would bite, or the ones that did were too slippery to reel in.

She sighed and pulled it in anyway, resting the rod against the cabin wall in defeat. Nausea was beginning to churn in her stomach from the constant swaying, and her exhaustion wasn't helping, either. "I think I'll stick to music."

"It takes a while to get the hang of." Amber's lips were downturned in concentration, her expression hewn from stone as she reeled the line back in. "I'm almost out of bait anyway."

"So what was your mother like?" Drew couldn't keep herself from asking. She had always been rapt at the idea of parents, perhaps because she had never had any of her own. "I'd love to hear about her."

Amber's jaw clenched. "I don't really want to talk about her."

"It must be difficult," she pushed. "Being out here, being reminded of her all the time."

The look that Amber shot Drew might have

sliced through her completely for all of its sharp, cold ire. And yet Drew wanted to know her, wanted to know everything about her. She wouldn't give up on her yet.

She didn't have a choice; Amber pointed across the sea, cutting Drew off before she could ask anything more. "Dolphins."

Drew wouldn't have noticed the small gray masses leaping across the water without Amber's keen eye, and yet it was true: dolphins danced across the choppy waves not too far from them. A laugh of awe escaped Drew as she gripped the edge of the boat with both hands. "I had no idea we even had dolphins in these seas."

"Whales, too." Amber nodded with a small smile that softened the tension that had passed between them a moment ago. Her presence was Drew's only source of warmth. God, she was freezing now, her bones shaking uncontrollably and her lips numb. For a moment, though, she did not think about that. For a moment, she merely watched the dolphins and imagined how it must feel to be so free. When she turned her head, she found that she was being watched, too.

"You must see so much out here," Drew said, tucking back a piece of hair that had escaped her bun self-consciously. She understood, now, why Amber had chopped all hers off. The briny breeze was a sticky balm tangling her stray waves. It would be a nightmare to drag a brush through later.

"It's never a dull moment." Amber fiddled with the zip on her raincoat. "What about you, though? Where do you live when you're not in Edna?"

Drew hadn't lived anywhere in over a year, but she only shrugged and said, "Here and there."

"You said you used to live in the city. Which one?"

"I've been up and down," Drew replied, swallowing down bile. The ceaseless swaying... it was churning up her lunch and the alcohol from the night before. "London, Manchester, Liverpool."

Amber's brows knitted together, cheeks rosy from the burn of the wind. "What about your family?"

A ragged breath escaped Drew, and she could no longer look Amber in the eye. Her seasickness wasn't getting any better, either, and the last thing she wanted to do was throw up all over *Diane*. She felt the nausea draining her face of its color, drying out her lips and her mouth and leaving a bad taste in its stead. "I don't —"

Amber's hand found her back. Drew would have relished her touch had she not been on the brink of vomiting. "Are you all right?"

"Feeling a little bit seasick." She sucked in a deep breath to settle her heaving stomach. Couldn't the waves sit still beneath the hull for even a moment? "I'll be okay."

"Sit down." Amber forced Drew down on the bench before handing her a flask. "Drink this.

It's tea."

The thought of something bitter in her mouth only made her feel worse, but she obeyed — not that she was given much of a choice, with Amber pressing it to her lips. It was still warm, and that, at least, soothed her throat and eased her shivering a little.

"Sorry," Drew apologized weakly. "I've never been on a boat before."

"It happens to the best of us," Amber replied, voice soft enough that Drew felt slightly better. Her hands tracing soothing circles across her spine might have sent sparks running through her if she weren't feeling so ill. "My brother used to throw up everywhere when he first started coming out here. He had to wear my dad's shirt once because he ruined his own. It drowned him to the point where we had to tie up the sleeves to keep him from tripping up."

Drew choked out a laugh. "I'll try not to do the same."

"You're okay." Amber gave her shoulder a squeeze, forcing another sip down her. "I'll get us back to shore as quick as I can. If you need to throw up, do it in this."

A paper bag was swapped for the flask, and Drew gave Amber an appreciative nod. "Thanks."

The motor rumbled to life again in an instant, and that sound alone made Drew want to throw up. She managed to make it back to the harbor without embarrassing herself too much, though, Amber helping her off the boat as she battled with legs that would not obey her commands.

"I'm so sorry," she repeated on more than one occasion.

Not once did Amber make her feel like a burden, though, as she led her across the bridge to a small white house tucked away on the bay.

Eighteen

Amber's house was all shadows and old furniture, as though Drew had stepped into the past upon passing the welcome mat by the door. It wouldn't be the first time this weekend that the past had found her.

It was quiet, too, so that every creak and shudder of the house settling could be heard as long as they weren't talking — which they weren't. But then the kettle began to shriek, and as Amber stood at the counter with her back to Drew, she took the opportunity to examine the pictures on the wall. Most of them were of a light-haired woman she didn't recognize, though she could see the same icy eyes had been passed down to Amber.

Diane. All smiles and warmth.

She must have been a lot to miss.

"I'm sorry," Drew said, clearing her throat when it came out all cracked. "For ruining the afternoon."

The kettle's whistle quieted. Amber picked it up, poured, stirred the tea before she responded. "You didn't ruin anything." When she turned around, her expression was softer than Drew had been expecting. "How are you feeling?"

The tightening in Drew's chest eased ever so slightly. "Better. Thank you."

Amber pulled the tea bags out. They were not the usual brown that Drew was used to, and, when Amber slid the steaming cup across the kitchen table to her, neither was the drink itself. She frowned down at it, the faint smell of citrus burning her nose along with something stronger, spicier.

"My mum always used to make us this when we got back — especially if Kit was sick. Ginger and lemon." Amber blew on the hot tea before setting her mug down and sitting in the chair adjacent to Drew. "Settles the stomach."

Drew smiled softly, though she could still feel her feet swaying. Her limbs had not yet realized they were no longer on the boat. She took a sip, the tea scalding her tongue, and grimaced. The sharpness of the ginger made it even worse than Rusty's usual lemon-and-honey concoction.

Amber laughed. "It's disgusting, isn't it?"

"It's, er…" Drew wrestled for the right word. "Different."

"You don't have to drink it. You do get used to it, though, after a few sips."

Drew drank again, if only to prove that she appreciated the gesture. "Despite my weak stomach, I had a good time today. Thank you."

Amber's slight smile lingered as her eyes locked on Drew's, so unexpectedly that her breath caught. They were as silver as the gray light pouring across them from the window above the sink, and, for once, not so guarded or cold. No, they were light — friendly, even.

"I had a good time too," Amber responded quietly, wrapping her fingers around her mug. "It's been a long time since I last sailed with anyone else. It was nice not to be alone."

You never have to be alone, Drew wanted to say. *Not anymore.* She clamped the words down with her lips before they fell out too carelessly. Amber reached out her hand, the pad of her thumb grazing Drew's cheekbone. Drew stilled, afraid that if she moved even an inch she would frighten Amber away.

"Eyelash," Amber explained in a whisper. It was true that when she pulled her thumb away, a small black hair was stuck there. Drew still could not move, could not breathe, in the absence of her touch, not until Amber blew the eyelash away and returned to her tea with flushed cheeks.

She wanted more, wanted Amber's touch to linger and pepper itself across every inch of her, wanted that cord tied around her stomach to stop tugging so insistently every time Amber pulled it taut. More than that, she wanted Amber to remember, as Mabel had said she might. She wanted her to feel the same way.

"Are you free tomorrow?" The question burst from her before she could think.

"I ..." Amber hesitated. "I can make myself free. What did you have in mind?"

"Do you know any lakes nearby?" It was a long shot, and she was probably being foolish by buying into any of it at all, but if Drew could just trigger Amber's memories the way that Mabel had suggested

"Lakes?" Amber's brows furrowed. "Why a lake?"

Drew shook her head at her own absurdity. "Never mind. I was just thinking of somewhere different, is all."

Amber worried at her lip, fingers dancing across the rim of her mug. Drew had seen her do that before, in another life: red-painted nails swirling around the edge of a champagne flute. The visions — the memories — were clearer now, clearer every time she saw Amber, and for once, she did not feel as though she were going insane. She could feel it between them — the knot that had always tied them together, both in this life and in others.

All Drew needed was for Amber to feel it too.

"I think I know a place," Amber said finally, just when Drew was beginning to think she had blown it.

Drew's heart fluttered, and suddenly the pocket watch did not feel like a heavy burden in her jacket pocket. "Yeah?"

Amber's hand found Drew's across the table. "Yeah," she said.

Nineteen

Drew halted in the hallway so quickly that Amber nearly collided with her back. It was already getting dark outside, and her family would no doubt be back soon — the only reason she had been leading Drew out at all. The truth was that she could have spent so many more hours with her.

It was her mother's old piano that Drew's dark eyes were fixed on, though it was gathering dust and soaked in shadows beneath the staircase.

"Do you play?" Drew asked, fingers swiping across the keys as though she couldn't help herself.

"No," Amber replied, an ache seizing her chest as she thought of all the times her mother's fingers had pressed those same ivory keys. Now it just sat untouched, sheet music remaining open on the last song she had ever played: a melody she could no longer remember hearing. "My mother did."

"Oh." Drew's hand fell from the piano as though it were coated in some sort of contagious disease, regret swelling in her features. "I'm sorry."

Amber shook her head and pressed one of the keys. It had fallen out of tune, sounding more like the first breath of somebody who had just been resuscitated than anything else. "There's nothing to be sorry for. You're welcome to play it, if you'd like."

"I couldn't —"

"You could," Amber urged. "I'm sure she'd be glad to know someone around here was actually using it."

Drew's gaze flitted between the piano and Amber reluctantly, and then she pulled the stool out in surrender and sat in front of the keys.

Amber joined her, her elbow brushing against Drew's as she blew away the dust and nearly choked the both of them in the process. "Do you play often?"

"I used to." Her voice was as low and reson-ant as a purr as she played a quick, tinkling melody to warm herself up. "It's kind of hard when you live in a van, though. I have to take any opportunity I can find."

Drew's fingers hovered restlessly, nails chipped and painted black. Amber couldn't help but imagine interlacing her own between them again as she had at the table, feeling the calluses of her palm and kissing away the blisters. Drew's presence was a suffocating, inescapable thing that wrapped her up in invisible arms and took her somewhere new. The more time she spent with her, the more she yearned for more.

"Let's see," Drew murmured in deliberation. "Any requests?"

"Whatever comes to you. Play me something you love."

It was all the permission Drew needed. Amber vaguely recognized the melody, but it wasn't one her mother had ever played for her. No, this was all Drew, with some sections lingering, longing, and others rich crescendos that had Amber's heart stuttering in time with the tune. It wasn't the sound that made her breath catch in her throat, but the way Drew's eyelids shuttered halfway, the way her lips puckered and her soul, body, weaved itself into the music. It filled this hollow and empty house with light until it was spilling with it, until they were no longer beneath the darkness of the staircase, sitting among ghosts, but somewhere golden and alive. It was not like watching her play the drums. That had been violent and raw. This... this was magic.

It brought with it images of angels and devils, pearls and diamonds, champagne. A toothy smile and a heady perfume. A glimpse of a life Amber did not know.

If she could play like that on an old piano in need of tuning, god only knew what she could do somewhere else.

Amber felt stripped bare when Drew had finished, her mouth gaping as Drew came to with a few, jagged breaths. Blinking, Amber turned to her. Drew licked her lips, surprise flickering in her eyes as though she, too, couldn't believe what had just taken place.

"That was..." Amber breathed, at a loss for

words. "You play beautifully."

"I'm a little rusty." She smiled wryly, letting her hands fall from the keys and into her lap.

"No," Amber said. "No, you were perfect." She felt like a fool, tripping over her words as her clammy hands fidgeted with her sleeves. They were sitting so close on the bench. Had they always been, or had Drew drawn her in slowly during the song?

"I've missed it." Drew eyed the piano solemnly. "I love the drums but... I don't know, the piano —"

"Is your first love?" Amber finished. She could see it in her, see the way it radiated from her like smoke. The piano set her on fire. The piano was her heart and soul.

"Something like that, yeah," she murmured.

"Then why not quit the band and do something with it? You should be playing in theaters or recording albums or something."

Drew shrugged, but her dark eyes were still flickering with glowing embers left over from playing. "I never knew how to get into it, get noticed."

"If you play like that, someone is bound to notice you." Amber's hands found Drew's, her thigh warm against her skin. "I would."

"Would you?" Drew whispered, throat bobbing as she swallowed.

Amber only nodded, eyes falling to her lips. She wanted to kiss her, but didn't know how. A part of her, the part that shielded her away with glass walls, kept her defenses up, reminding her that Drew would be leaving soon. The other part didn't care; the other part of her knew that this was right, no matter how long it lasted or how it would end.

Drew leaned in before Amber had decided which one to listen to, and the glass wall shattered in front of her. Her lips were far softer than her hands. Amber could taste the lemon on her tongue from the tea they had sipped earlier, and the salt, too, from the sea. Blood pulsed in Amber's ears as Drew's tongue pushed against the seam of her lips, asking permission. Amber answered by parting them, giving herself to Drew completely until they had melded into a tangle of rough breaths and desperate touches. She wanted all of her, wanted to feel every part of her with her lips and her fingers and her hips.

Amber had lost herself in Drew. She did not want to be found. Everything was familiar, and everything was right.

Like coming home.

Twenty

Amber didn't remember; that much had been clear. Yet they had shared something — something new, something that Drew had not felt in any other vision or memory or dream. Something even better, perhaps.

Drew's lips still tingled with the memory of her as she trudged up Ethan's driveway, the sheep bleating at her as though she were a trespasser. Her bandmates were packing up the van, with Ethan helping them, and her stomach sank.

She couldn't leave. Not yet. Not until Amber remembered too.

"She returns," Rusty exclaimed by way of greeting as she nestled her guitar in its case and clicked it closed. The rest of the band eyed her suspiciously. Max still had fake blood smeared on her neck and Zandra's eyes were smudged with black. Rusty was the only one who looked relatively fresh. And Ethan —

Well, Ethan looked even worse than Drew must have on Amber's boat. He was practically green, with sunglasses perched on his head. Drew was glad she had stayed clear of him and his cocktails last night.

"Where've you been, stranger?" Max asked, chewing noisily on a piece of gum as Drew reached them.

"Just with a friend," Drew said, waving them off in dismissal. "Are you heading off to-night?"

"*We*," Rusty emphasized with a frown, "are heading off as soon as we pack up. If you need to say your goodbyes to that fiery blonde pixie you've been ogling, you'd better do it quickly."

"Wait." Ethan slid his sunglasses off, puzzled eyes flitting to Drew. "What blonde pixie?"

Drew's face flushed with heat, but she kept her composure, ignoring Ethan's question completely. "What if we stayed another day or two? We don't have any shows lined up until next weekend now."

"I only know one fiery blonde pixie," Ethan continued, stepping in front of Drew so that her vision of her bandmates was obscured, "and she so happens to be my best friend."

"We're not staying," Rusty answered, as though Ethan hadn't spoken. "This place is boring and we need to get back to the city. Sorry if that interrupts your little love affair."

"Drew Dawson, are you having a love affair with my best friend?" Ethan questioned, his hand falling to his chest in shock.

"It's not a love affair." Drew rolled her eyes and pushed him to the side so that she could see the band again. "Look, I just want to stick around for a few days more. Please?"

"Then what is it?" Ethan asked.

"No." Rusty crossed her arms, expression taut with stubbornness. She was used to people obeying her every order and every wish as the lead singer. Not today, though. This town — or, rather, one person in it — was pulling Drew to stay, and she had to listen. "We agreed we would stay the weekend for you. Now it's time to leave."

"What's a few more days?"

"Can somebody please tell me what on earth is going on?" Ethan chimed in frantically.

"There's nothing to do here!" Rusty argued. "I need to book us some more gigs in the city before we run out of money. I can't do that here. Plus we're all bored to tears and I'm sick of being woken up by a cock first thing in the bloody morning."

"His name is Terrence," Ethan said.

"I wasn't talking about Terrence." Rusty smiled sweetly, wickedness resting in the curve of her lips. "I was talking about you."

Ethan glowered.

"There are pubs here. You'll find something." Drew was pleading now, and she had to fight the urge to clasp her hands together in prayer. "Please, Rusty. A few more days. This is important to me."

Rusty huffed and glanced at Zandra and Max. Neither of them seemed particularly interested in the conversation, and the fact that they were still packing said enough. They wouldn't stay, even if Drew got on her hands and knees and begged.

"Sorry, Drew." She shrugged finally, leaning against the camper. "We're leaving. If you want to make a stop along the way, we can, but we're not staying."

"I am." The words came out shaky, weak, but Drew still said them loud enough for them all to hear. "I'm staying."

Rusty raised an eyebrow. "And how will you get home?"

"I don't have a home," Drew replied. "That's the problem."

"All of this for a fucking girl." Rusty shook her head angrily and climbed into the driver's seat. The door slammed shut with so much force that Drew felt it resonating in her chest like an explosion. She didn't regret her decision, though — not when Max and Zandra climbed into the back with uncertain waves of goodbye, or when Rusty began to blast the music from the radio, or when the campervan circled Ethan's large driveway, tires chafing against gravel, before leaving Drew in the dust.

She regretted it only a little when she remembered that Ethan was still standing next to her.

"Drew Dawson, are you or are you not hooking up with my best friend?"

"No, Ethan Moors," Drew drawled, "I am not hooking up with her."

"But?" he urged.

Drew sighed. "But we did kiss."

"Oh my god," Ethan gasped dramatically. "And you were going to tell me when?"

"About the same time I asked you if I could stay with you for a few days," she offered.

Ethan only looked at her stonily with an expression that said *No details, no place to stay*.

"Look, there's something between us. I don't know what it is." She reached into her pocket and gripped the pocket watch. It was warm and clammy, like her hands; she had held it all the way home. "All I know is that I'd like to find out before I leave. Is that okay with you?"

Ethan's lips curved into a smile, an excited glint in his eye. "As long as you tell me everything, I think we can work something out, yes."

Drew shook her head with a smirk. "Good. Then we have a deal."

"Yes, we do," Ethan said, grinning.

Twenty-One

"I remember you."

Sidney sees Grace clearly for the first time as she untangles herself from his sheets and slides on her red silk slip dress. The fringe rattles, the sequins leaving faint red scratches down her face and her neck as she tugs it down over her bare, golden body. The body he had just touched every inch of with desperate hands, the body he had kissed up and down until his mouth ached. The memory sends heat searing between his legs again.

The empty space has turned cold beside him, and he has to force himself not to pull her back into bed with him. He wants to, though, wants another taste of the devil. The devil who had been a wolf once, and a farmgirl before that. He remembers now, clear as day. It has taken him all night, but heaven does he remember.

Aishling. Claude. Grace. The names are faint whispers, but they are hers. He remembers himself, too, always holding the pocket watch that now sits on his bedside table. A traveler. A thief. A pianist.

He doesn't know how it is possible. Perhaps he is hallucinating. Perhaps someone slipped something in his drink.

Or perhaps they were meant to find one another tonight.

"That's always a bonus after sex," she replies, voice husky enough to make his stomach twitch with wanting.

"No, I mean that I remember you from the last time we met." He pulls himself into a sitting position, the sheets rippling down to reveal his bare torso.

"When was that?" She slides her shoes on carefully before turning to him.

"At a ball in Paris. I stole your pocket watch." Sidney picks it up and drops it into her palm.

Grace merely glances at it before scoffing, her black hair curtaining her face. "I've never been to Paris, pretty boy. You got the wrong girl."

"You weren't a girl then." He can hear himself now as though through someone else's ears, and knows how stupid he sounds. But she was there too. She has to remember him. "Your name is on this watch, see." He points to the faint inscription. "Claude Augustin."

Grace narrows her eyes at him warily, and somehow that piercing scowl shrinks him down, makes him small. Is he wrong? Has he been wrong about this the whole time? "Were you drinking somethin' stronger than whiskey last night?"

"C'mon, Grace," he pleads, gathering the sheets so that he can scoot closer to her without exposing himself. She shifts away from him and the watch until she reaches the end of the bed, and then stands with her hands on her hips. She's tall — as tall as him, *almost. A giant in comparison to him while he sits like a fool in her shadow. What has he done? "You haven't wondered why I felt so familiar to you?"*

"I've probably seen you around town."

"I don't live in town." It's true: the room is a hotel room, with mismatched furniture and flimsy curtains only half hiding the view of Chicago away. In the corner, his shirts and trousers spill out of a black case. "Will you sit down? Let's talk about this."

"We're done talkin'," she mutters, gathering her purse and smoothing her hair down at the mirror. "I shoulda known better than to come back here with you."

Each word is a jab to his chest. "Grace, please."

"See ya, Sidney. Maybe we'll meet again in Timbuktu — let's say the year 2040. I'll be a polar bear, you'll be a mermaid." She leaves before he can respond, slamming the door shut behind her. Sidney's ears ring in the silence, and he sags, burying his face in his hands.

He had been so certain that he'd known her, that he'd loved her in another life. In two other lives, at the very least. Now she is gone, and there will be no way of fixing this.

Sunken into the mattress beside him, the pocket watch begins to tick again: his only company in the dark hotel room.

The dream had set Drew on edge. Unease had writhed in her the whole time that she had sat beside Amber in the passenger seat of her old Jeep, until eventually they had rolled to a stop in a large, empty carpark. Woods surrounded them on all sides, the leaves an array of marigold yellow and deep red that reminded Drew of the forest she had walked through to find Aishling in 1717. The forest where she had first found the watch.

Indeed, Amber had kept to her promise. The lake was only a ten-minute walk on a pathway of pine needles and damp soil. It was not exactly the pool of water Aishling had been washing her linens in, but it was good enough. A waterfall burbled over the rocks at one end so that the lake reflected the trees in distorted ripples on its surface, and it was murky where the silt had been disrupted from its bed at the bottom.

"Here we are," Amber said. "As requested."

"It's beautiful," Drew replied quietly, taking it in as Amber shrugged off her backpack and pulled out a tartan picnic blanket. "Thank you for bringing me here."

"Don't thank me yet," she warned, spreading the blanket before pulling out enough sandwiches to feed a small army. "It's supposed to rain soon."

"Then we'll get wet." Drew allowed herself a small smile despite the dread roiling in her stomach. As though sensing it, Amber stopped and tangled her fingers through her own, pulling her down onto the blanket.

"I'd be okay with that." Amber crossed her legs, dropping Drew's hand to unwrap a sandwich. "So when do you leave with the band?"

Drew averted her gaze to the lake, kicking her legs out in front of her and playing with a crisp brown leaf that floated across the blanket. "Actually... the band left yesterday."

Amber stopped, brows furrowing. "Without you?"

Drew nodded soberly. It hadn't seemed like a mistake yesterday, but now she couldn't help but wonder what she was doing. Amber might not remember, might think her insane for even suggesting that they had met before.

From the corner of her eye, Drew observed Amber's expression to see if the lake had reawakened anything in her, but all she found was concern.

"Why?"

"I..." Drew hesitated, sucking in a breath. How could Amber not see it yet? How could she not remember them, the farmer and the traveler? "I wasn't ready to leave."

You. I wasn't ready to leave you. It was left unsaid, but Amber still shuffled closer to her, placing a hand on her thigh. "Well, I'm glad you didn't."

Drew let her eyes fall shut, their foreheads kissing as she wrapped herself in Amber. She was of the earth: fresh, with the scent of rain and mint sticking to her skin, her clothes. Like Aishling. Like home.

Amber's fingers twisted themselves in her loose curls as they kissed slowly, steadily, savoring every lick and every bite, every moment they sank into one being. Not like yesterday — that had been frantic and new and necessary. No, this was something else entirely: a surrender, perhaps. A confirmation.

Drew didn't want it to end, didn't want to scare her away the way Sidney had scared away Grace, and yet she could feel herself pulling away as she realized that kissing Amber was kissing all of them. She could not look at Amber without seeing Grace, Claude, Aishling. Just as they were tethered to each other, they were also tethered to those versions of themselves.

It didn't feel right to be with Amber when Drew was the only one who understood what it truly meant.

Amber did not seem to realize, because her hands brushed down her arms, her waist, until they were pulling on a loose thread of her sweater. "Can I? I hate these things."

Drew nodded, because she could do nothing else, the thread snagging her jumper taut before snapping. She thought that would be the end of it, but Amber lifted Drew's right hand and tied the thread around her finger.

It was just a gesture, an absent one that Amber had probably not thought about at all, and yet it felt as though Drew's world was beginning again with just that piece of thread. So she found another one to pull and did the same, letting her thumb graze the soft parts of Amber's hands as she tied the knot around her same finger.

"We match," Drew murmured, and then, because she could not resist, she kissed that very thread on Amber's finger as though sealing it shut — the cord that had been pulling them together, coming to life in the form of a thin strand of fiber.

It would be her making.

It would be her undoing.

Drew pulled away and gathered a ragged breath, trembling fingers clawing into the soil. She had to do this, but she had to do it right this time. She had to be cautious, gentle, not as she had been last time, when they had rushed into it all.

"Do you believe in past lives, Amber?"

Amber frowned, licking her lips as though wanting to taste what Drew had left behind. "What?"

"Do you think that we could have been other people once, living different lives?"

Amusement glittered in her eyes. "I told you not to visit Mabel. She comes out with all sorts of spiritual crap."

A pang of disappointment sliced through Drew's stomach. Amber seemed not to notice, offering a sandwich to Drew.

"What if..." Drew tore her hands through her hair. What the hell was she doing — again?

Why couldn't she just let it slide, ignore it, be happy here with Amber instead of caught up in old memories that might not even belong to her? "What if I do believe in it?"

"Then I will just have to tease the shit out of you every time you bring it up," Amber joked, but when Drew didn't laugh, her eyes narrowed. "What's this about, Drew?"

In a last-ditch attempt, Drew pulled the pocket watch out and set it in Amber's hands. Her pale fingers brushed across the engraving in inspection, eyes reducing to slits.

"Does this look familiar to you?"

"Should it?" Amber asked, opening it up to examine the face.

Yes. Please remember. Please. "Am I still familiar to you, Amber? Does it still feel like we've known each other for longer than a few days?"

Amber's expression turned cold. "What are you trying to do here?"

"I'm trying to figure it out," Drew said, voice rising in desperation. "I'm trying to figure *us* out. How can you not remember? How can you not feel it?"

"Feel what?"

"*Everything*," she breathed, tears filling her eyes. It had been building in her for days, this confusion, this intensity, this desire. Now it mingled with the frustration of not being understood, remembered. What was the point in any of it if she couldn't share it with the one person she was supposed to? "Everything we were. Everything we've ever been. We met..."

Drew trailed off at the look of irritation and utter bewilderment on Amber's face. It was no use. She didn't remember. She didn't remember the lake, or the watch, or her. Everything that had triggered Drew's memories and dreams... they had done nothing for her. And if this weekend hadn't done it, with Halloween and the horses, the music, what would?

She was a fool. Had always been a fool. Perhaps that was just how it was meant to be. Perhaps Mabel had been wrong.

"Look, I like you, Drew," Amber said, "I do. But you're still not much more than a stranger to me, and you're not making any sense."

"No." She nodded, ice dripping into her hollow stomach. "No, I'm not. I'm sorry."

Amber chewed on her bottom lip. Drew couldn't look at her anymore, so she stood up on weak legs and dusted down her jeans. Rejection was an oily beast that slithered in her gut.

"We should go."

"Drew —"

She didn't stick around to hear the end of Amber's sentence. Didn't want to spend another moment knowing that everything she had said, felt, seen, had been unrequited and unreturned.

It was time to leave.

Twenty-Two

Amber should have said something. Anything. Instead she'd driven in silence. And when she came to park outside of Ethan's, Drew did not stick around to wish her a goodbye.

Regret wriggled beneath her skin. Regret and confusion. Nothing made sense with Drew.

Nothing had ever made sense with Drew.

A lie.

Everything had made sense with Drew.

Now she was gone, and Amber couldn't get her back.

Twenty-Three

The waves roiled beneath the pier. Drew watched them in a trance, gripping the pocket watch in her hand. She had checked it once, twice, thrice, but it was still broken, still stuck on ten thirty. Perhaps that should have given her hope, but she had seen this before, in other lives, with other people.

It was time to put an end to it.

She put every ounce of force into her throw. The pocket watch tumbled into the sea, the surface too rough for her to see where it landed beneath the sea foam.

Good.

She would not be its prisoner a second longer. She had spent lifetimes doing that already.

She was not a soul mate, and she was not a victim of fate. She was Drew Dawson, and she would leave this behind her without looking back.

No more waiting for something she could not reach.

No more.

Part II

Edinburgh, 2020: The Last Goodbye

Twenty-Four

If she were to admit it, Amber did not despise the city quite as much as she had expected. It was okay, really, if she got used to the constant honking of car horns and the fact that it rained and hailed far more often than in Whitby — and that was saying something.

Kit had been begging her for a good four years to visit Edinburgh over Christmas, and, finally, here she was. Finally she had put her pride aside enough to agree.

The fact that her father had packed her suitcase and locked her in the Jeep before she could change her mind only had a little to do with it.

Still, it had made her brother and her father happy. She was even warming to Emily, who hovered beside her now as though afraid she might take off in the middle of the street.

"I'm so glad you're here," she said, not for the first time, as John and Kit ambled in front of them. Tonight they were going to watch a concert — Emily's idea, when they had exhausted their list of daytime activities only three days in and had time to spare before Emily and Kit's engagement party on Saturday night.

"I'm glad too." Amber forced a smile, though it was not a complete lie. They came to a stop outside a large building, looming with its ancient architecture and pillars. The theater. There were no queues outside: the doors were already open, which saved them from standing and losing a limb in the dead of winter.

"Here we are." Kit grinned as he led them up the stone steps, pulling the tickets from his pocket. "Emily and I love this place. So much better than one of those grotty little bars that put on rock concerts, isn't it, Emily?"

Amber happened to like those grotty little bars, and so had Kit once, too. They had filled the miniature hole that Drew had left three years ago, reminding her of the drummer she had lost herself in for a short time. The drummer who had left her.

Amber still had to remind herself that it had only been a weekend, not a lifelong love affair. It had felt like so much more. How could she still think of her, three years on? Why couldn't she forget?

Amber shook off the familiar ache in her chest and let Emily drag her up the stairs, showing the tickets to the usher at the door. Her father cast her an uncertain glance over his shoulder. He, too, appreciated the occasional rock concert. This place was certainly not built for headbanging and cheap drinks.

No, it was a fancy, carpeted place with golden chandeliers lighting the lobby and the inescapable smell of newness — rather than ale — chasing them through the marbled entrance. Amber felt underdressed, even with her coat covering her plain black shirt and trousers. She could not hide the worn Converse on her feet, though, especially not when Emily towered over her in stilettos. Perhaps she should have wiped her grimy soles on the mat before entering.

She was glad when Kit led them into the theater, hushed voices carrying across as the darkness as others searched for their seats. Kit didn't have that problem. He had gotten the tickets from his boss — a stuck-up, arrogant man, he said, but at least that arrogance had bought him seats at the front — velvet-lined seats at that, Amber noted as they found their seat number. Kit and Emily sandwiched her, with her father at the end of the aisle; good. He would no doubt be snoring loud enough to put the trombonists to shame before the music even began.

"What exactly are we watching tonight?" Amber asked, whispering, though the show had not started yet. Still, the seats were filling up and she could already imagine the snotty people in the row behind hushing her if she so much as breathed too loudly.

"The New Edinburgh Orchestra," he responded, handing her a program that had been wedged between the chairs.

Amber glanced over it with little interest. "Perhaps after the show we can dine on caviar and discuss the pros and cons of different champagne flutes."

"Oh, be quiet." Kit rolled his eyes and snatched the program back. "You used to like it when Mum played the classics."

It was true that Diane would have preferred this much more, would probably have watched the entire show on the edge of her seat, especially when they were only a few feet away from the stage. Before Amber could say that, though, the lights dimmed and the curtains peeled back, revealing an orchestra of shadows.

The spotlight centered on them, the conductor at the front counting them in, and then music was all that Amber could hear, see, taste. It thrummed in her, the different instruments sharp and new as they melded together, swirled above the theater, above everything. She could barely breathe for it.

Amber's eyes instinctively fell to the piano, to the place where her mother, too, would have focused.

Her heart stopped beating. Her blood stopped circulating. Because she knew the girl sitting on the stool. Drew.

Drew, playing with her eyes half-closed and her fingers working tirelessly, body jolting as she moved up and down the piano. The other instruments faded out. There was only her, playing the keys, wearing a black suit and looking for all the world like the professional Amber had always known she could have been — *was*. Her hair was a silken curtain falling across her shoulder, her mouth a heart-shaped pout with the tip of her tongue peeking out in concentration.

She was where she was supposed to be.

And she did not even know that Amber sat mere feet away, watching, suffocating.

Amber might have relaxed and tried to enjoy it, but her stomach began to churn with something foreign, shadows dotting the corners of her vision.

∞∞∞

A pianist with angel wings strapped around his shoulders, all brown, speckled skin and golden light, playing a song to only her. She could watch him all night and never tire of the way his dainty fingers graze the keys, the way the white feathers on his back ruffle with each chord, the way he smiles to himself as though nothing else exists.

The saccharine taste of champagne sits on her tongue, fringe and sequins from her dress grazing the parts of her that remain uncovered: knees, arms, neck. Red glitters in her peripheral vision, but she is too lost in him to be distracted.

His dark curls bob in the reflection cast on the smooth piano top, soft features mirrored there. If it weren't Halloween, if the room weren't filled with costumed dancers, she might truly believe that he is heaven-sent.

He does not even notice her as she approaches.

∞∞∞

Amber stood from her seat as though she were still living it now, still watching him. Perhaps she was.

Kit gripped her wrist, tugging her down. She ignored him. She wouldn't sit yet. She wanted Drew to see her, to know that she was here in the front row... but Drew only squinted into the bright light as she finished the first piece, and Amber knew that she was nothing but mere shadows to her.

She could not see her — and even if she did, what would Amber say? It had been three years.

"Amber, what are you doing?" Kit scolded, eyes crinkling in confusion. His hushed voice was a distant thing that did not reach her completely, not above the applause. "Sit down."

Amber's stomach ached with the desperation, the raw desire, to talk to Drew. She took a shaky step toward her, still halfway between another life, another memory that was not hers, where she was dressed as a devil and played the part well.

Kit pulled her back.

"Sit down," he whispered through gritted teeth.

This time she did. Still, her eyes did not stray from Drew for the rest of the performance; she existed always between the angelic man she did not know, and the woman who now sat in front of her.

Perhaps a part of Amber had always known she would find Drew again. Perhaps that same part of her had, at the very least, hoped. And here she was, now, sitting closer to Drew than she had been in three years.

How could it be possible?

Twenty-Five

Drew's bones still hummed with electricity as she spilled into the lobby. The balls of her feet throbbed from wearing such high heels all day, and she had to restrain herself from kicking them off as their sharp points plunged into the red carpet like daggers. The others had gone out to celebrate opening night, but all Drew wanted was to sink into bed and not rise until the sun woke her tomorrow morning so that she could do this all again.

That plan was soon forgotten as she glimpsed a blonde woman she had never expected to see again sitting on one of the sofas by the entrance.

Amber.

Amber, wan and shaky and sitting in front of her somehow, waiting.

But that was impossible. Drew had thrown away the pocket watch, and it was not Halloween, the time when they had always found one another before. How could she be here now? How had she found her?

"Hi," Amber breathed, taking an apprehensive step toward Drew. Her voice echoed off the stone walls eerily. The lobby had emptied save for them and the cleaner mopping the floor by the grand staircase with his earphones on. It might as well have been a dream, a hallucination, with no one else here to witness it, prove it.

Her hair, though — her hair was chopped closely to her head, now, and was the neater for it. It exposed her dainty, heart-shaped face and laid her birthmark bare — god, Drew had missed that face, that birthmark that told her no matter what had happened, it had been real.

Other than that, Amber looked no different, with her pink rosebud lips, her jutting chin, her piercing eyes that always seemed to surpass Drew's skin and bone and pass straight to her soul. Pixie-like. Perfect. *Amber*.

"Hello," Drew choked out, adjusting the straps of her shoulder bag uncertainly. She had been floating with the music minutes ago, and now everything seemed to weigh her down with impossible pressure. She had missed Amber — had even dreamed about moments like this, where she could tell her that she had become a pianist and it was all because of her encouragement. She had lain awake at night wondering if Amber could see the same stars that glowed outside the window of Drew's new apartment, had seen her in every falling leaf and every golden lock of hair. *Amber*. Even now it was both the name that whistled through her veins and the color of her shattered soul. But Amber did not feel the same. Amber did not remember, and all her being here did was hurt. Her birthmark, the birthmark that had somehow followed her in all of her forms, was a stark reminder of that, too.

"I..." Amber loosed an uneven breath, and then a light, embarrassed laugh. "It's been a long time."

"Yes, it has." Drew nodded, still not daring to move. "You cut your hair."

Amber ran her fingers through a golden tuft self-consciously, leaving it to curl up at the top. "I got sick of it — again."

"I like it that way." Drew breathed in through her nose — it felt like the first breath she had taken since seeing her. "Why are you here, Amber?"

"My brother lives here," she replied. "We're visiting to celebrate an early Christmas together, and he wanted to see a show, and — I had no idea you'd be here until I saw you on stage. I was front row."

That at least brought Drew some comfort: she'd had no family to invite, no friends. Knowing that Amber had been sitting front row at her first real show was... well, it was everything. It made her feel not so alone on that vast stage.

"I live here, too. Have done for about a year now."

"What are the chances?" Amber's smile was strained, light eyes glittering. As though forgetting her short hair, she tucked a nonexistent strand behind her ear.

Drew gulped. What *were* the chances? This was not how it usually happened with them. This was not how it had ever happened before.

Had throwing the pocket watch into the sea thrown with it the way in which they were bound? Was this really a mere coincidence, untethered to anything that Drew had remembered or experienced three years ago?

"It's a small world, I suppose," Drew said, as nonchalantly as she could.

"You were…" Amber bit her lip, took another step forward. "Well, you belong up there. You really do."

"It has a lot to do with you, actually. You made me think I could, so I did. Thank you for that — for listening to me play that day." Her mouth still tingled with the kiss they had shared after Drew had played for Amber on the dusty piano. She hadn't been able to play that song since without thinking of her — and so had stopped playing it altogether, eventually.

Amber softened. "So you're not in the band anymore?"

Drew shook her head. "I never went back. Traveled around for a bit and then wound up here."

Amber seemed to remember where *here* was, and broke her gaze finally to cast her eyes to the carpet. "I never thought I'd see you again."

"I didn't think you ever wanted to," Drew answered, honesty raw in her tone. It was true: Amber could have walked away tonight with perhaps some closure at seeing Drew. Instead she had waited for her. Drew could still not gather why.

"I did. I regretted not saying goodbye, not…" Amber bit her lip. "I don't know. I was confused. I still am."

"Understandably," Drew allowed. "It got a bit weird, didn't it?"

Amber opened her mouth to reply, but another voice got there before her.

"For God's sake, Amber." A fair-haired man stood at the door, the cold air sweeping in as he held it open. Drew could see the resemblance to Amber, especially since their hair was practically the same length and style now: they could have been twins. She recognized him, too, from the pictures that had been hung on Amber's kitchen wall. "We're freezing out here."

Amber shot him a glare. "Go on without me, then."

"You don't know the way back," he argued.

"I'm sure I'll manage."

"I should let you go," said Drew, eyes flitting between the two of them. "It was nice to see you, Amber."

"No, wait," Amber pleaded, stunning Drew enough to stop her in her tracks. "Perhaps we could catch up sometime?"

"Wait," the man at the door said, stepping into the foyer now and letting the door fall shut behind him. His coat was dusted with hailstones, the tips of his hair damp and dripping. "Weren't you the pianist tonight?"

Drew gave a slight nod and forced a polite smile. "Drew Dawson."

"Wow." He blew out a breath of awe. "You were amazing. So talented. I'm Kit, Amber's brother."

He slid his gloves off quickly and held out a hand, which Drew took cautiously and shook. It was like ice, and she was more than glad when he dropped it back to his side. "Thank you."

"Drew and I are, er, old friends," Amber explained to Kit.

"Why didn't you say?" He furrowed his brows, the expression so much like Amber's that Drew thought she was seeing double. Even their eyes were the same, though Kit's were warmer, less intense. "We're having an early Christmas lunch tomorrow, if you'd like to join us."

"I wouldn't want to intrude," Drew replied, shooting a helpless look at Amber. Surely Amber did not want that, not after the last time they had spoken.

"You wouldn't be," Kit insisted, wringing his soggy hat in his hands. "The more the merrier, right, Amber?"

Amber pursed her lips, and then her eyes were back on Drew. She wanted to writhe away from the scrutiny.

"It would be nice to catch up with you, if you'd like," Amber said finally, bashfully.

Drew wilted in defeat. "Then that would be

lovely. Thanks."

"Great," Kit said. "Amber will give you the address, won't you, Amber?"

Amber already had a pen out, using the back of the concert program as a notepad.

"See you tomorrow, then?" It was a question rather than a statement, with what Drew could only decipher as hope dripping from it as she handed her the address.

"Tomorrow," Drew agreed, tucking the program into her blazer. And then Amber and Kit were walking away. Amber looked back at her only once on her way out, as though she could not quite believe that Drew was corporeal.

Drew couldn't believe it either.

Twenty-Six

Smoke still lingers from the bonfire, choking the Irish landscape with its dreary gray. She watches him saddle up his horse by the gate, red hair serving as the only respite from the monochromatic morning.

Shay. She remembers his name before she remembers her own. Everything about him is familiar: every part of him she has touched, kissed, loved.

He belongs here, with her. He is home.

"Don't go." The words are selfish, but she says them anyway. "Stay. Please."

"I wish I could." He steps away from the horse with a gentle pat to its mane, treading close enough to her that she can see the tears hiding in his green eyes. "Well, if we're wishing for things, I wish that you could come with me. See the world with me."

"Please," she pleads, hand curling around the nape of his neck. The waves of his hair brush her fingers, soothing her. "Stay, Shay."

"You know I can't," he whispers, a muscle feathering in his jaw as he swallows and bows his head to her. "In another life, perhaps. Another time." His absence leaves her cold as he pulls away to search his front pocket.

"Here." He drops the pocket watch he has been

trying to fix all weekend into her hand. It is cold, heavy, dead. "Hang on to it for me. Perhaps it'll help us find one another again someday."

She brushes a speck of dirt from the engraving with her thumb. "It doesn't even work."

"It worked for me," Shay mutters softly, branding a gentle, enduring kiss into her forehead. She can feel the mark still when he pulls away, stinging between her brows. She hopes it stays forever. "Come with me."

"I can't." The words are like knives on her tongue.

She should say goodbye now, or kiss him again, or plead with him to stay. Instead she only basks in the last few moments of him, until he drops her hand and climbs onto his mount. The horse grunts as though in its own version of farewell.

Shay tips his head to her with a sad smile, and her heart stutters. "Until we meet again, Aishling."

She nods, clutching the pocket watch to her heart as the horse begins to trot away from her, to where his brother waits by the edge of the woods. The hope Shay's words bring is the only thing that keeps her from falling apart.

"Until we meet again."

Only when Shay has disappeared into the thicket of dying trees does the pocket watch begin to tick to life — as though compensating for the fact that Aishling's own heart has stopped completely.

∞ ∞ ∞

Amber had been in a daze all morning, a ghost in the midst of all of Kit's and Emily's scurrying as they battled with pots and pans, gloopy gravy and burnt chicken. Her father, wisely, had hidden himself behind a newspaper on the couch, and resurfacing only when his brandy needed refilling. It was only Amber who did not have a place in the apartment, only Amber who had not slept well in the spare room, dreaming of farms and horses, pocket watches and Drew.

No, not Drew. Someone else. But they had felt like Drew, in a strange way. Possessed her warmth, looked at her the way Drew often had.

A knock at the door tugged her out of it all, and she was glad for the chance to escape the smell of sage and onion stuffing and Emily's constant huffing and sighing every time Kit put something on the plate too haphazardly or brought out the wrong knife to carve the meat. If they were still engaged to be married by the end of the day, it would be a miracle.

Anxiety swirled in Amber's stomach as she opened the door to find Drew hovering from foot to foot, as though debating whether she should run before she was caught.

Too late, now.

She held a bowl of trifle that looked...

melted, the layers collapsed and indistinguishable save for the thick pile of jelly on the bottom.

"Hello," Drew said, offering the trifle.

Amber took it gingerly. "You didn't have to bring anything."

"I probably shouldn't have, to be honest." Drew grimaced. "I've been trying to learn how to cook and bake now that I live alone. Clearly, it's not working too well."

"I'm sure it tastes better than it looks." Amber set it down on the foyer table and gathered her coat. "Do you mind if we go somewhere to talk first? Dinner isn't ready just yet, and…"

"Of course." Drew nodded, shoving her hands in her coat pockets. It was far from the scuffed leather she had once donned, this close to a blazer. Her boots were heeled, too, and she wore black tights rather than ripped jeans. So much had changed about her, and yet Amber's heart still stuttered and started for her. She was still Drew, still beautiful and full of fire. The drummer still lived somewhere beneath those fancy clothes.

They stepped out into the corridor — with Amber shutting the door quietly so that Kit would not immediately come running after her to demand where she was going — and descended the stairs in silence. The cold air sliced Amber as they spilled out onto the streets, Christmas lights twinkling in windows and garlands snaked around lampposts.

They walked without any sense of purpose,

taking slow and wary steps that had them almost falling into one another. Drew was even taller in her heeled boots. Amber felt like a dwarf in comparison.

"It's really good to see you, Drew," she began.

"Yeah?" Drew asked quietly, surprise flickering across her face.

"I thought about you a lot after you left. I shouldn't have left things the way I did."

Amber had thought about all of the things she could have said and done differently a million times over since that day. Drew had brought warmth and life back into her that weekend, and Amber had been left hollow when it had been taken — or pushed, if Amber was honest with herself — away too soon. She had not been able to find it — *feel* it — in anybody else since. "I wish it could have been different."

"I understand why it wasn't," Drew said with a timid nudge. "I'm sorry too, for the way I was."

"We're both different people now." Amber shrugged, biting down on her cheek.

"That we are," she agreed. "Are you still fishing?"

"I am. But I'm also helping out at the local angling school when I have the time."

"That sounds great." Drew kicked up an empty crisp packet, eyelashes black crescent moons on her high cheekbones. "How's Ethan?"

"Ethan is Ethan," Amber said wryly. "I don't see him too often anymore. He moved down south a few months ago with his new boyfriend. You can expect a wedding invite soon, I think."

"God help the man who decided to put up with him for life."

Amber laughed, but she was no longer thinking about Ethan. It was difficult to think about anything at all when she was walking beside Drew, their arms brushing. "I was thinking that maybe... it would be nice to spend some time with you before I go home, if you're free."

"I'd like that." Drew's cheeks dimpled as the corner of her mouth lifted. "I'd like that a lot."

"Good." Amber returned the smile, shifting slightly closer to her as the wind howled down the side street. Her cheeks stung with the cold, her fingers already losing sensation, and yet she might have stayed out here for hours if it meant getting Drew back.

If it meant getting all of it back.

Twenty-Seven

Drew had never eaten at a dining table, surrounded by family, before. For just a moment, while John complained that the mashed potatoes were too lumpy and Emily and Kit pulled a Christmas cracker, she could pretend that the family was her own and not someone else's.

"So how did the two of you meet?"

It was Emily who finally asked, motioning with her fork between Amber and Drew, who sat adjacent to one another. It might have been comfortable had she not noticed that Amber kept staring at her every time Drew turned her attention to the food on the plate. She had blown her nose and checked that no eyelashes had fallen onto her cheek self-consciously, but still Amber stared.

"Well," Amber began, chewing gingerly on a charred brussels sprout. Drew had left hers buried beneath her mash. "We met at the Halloween festival a few years back."

Drew nodded, swallowing her dry chicken with a grimace before she continued for Amber. "I was in one of the bands playing at the pavilion, and we shared a mutual friend — Ethan Moors." Drew hadn't heard from him in at least a year, but then, she hadn't heard from many people from her past recently.

"It seems like you have a lot of history," Kit observed, sipping his brandy and dabbing the corners of his mouth with his napkin. "How come you've never mentioned her before, Amber?"

"We just lost touch." Her eyes gleamed as she glanced over to Drew again. Drew cleared her throat uncomfortably in response.

"Do you live here in Edinburgh, Drew?"

"I do." She tore her gaze away from Amber long enough to answer. "I moved here a couple of years back."

"Good." Kit smiled, a warm, appreciative smile that surprised Drew. "That means Amber has another reason to drag herself up here more often."

The thought made Drew's stomach twist with longing, but she said nothing as she tucked into her meal again.

"Do you have family here?" Emily added.

"No, no family." Drew shook her head with a sad smile, shifting uncomfortably in her seat.

"Where do they live?"

"They don't." She gauged Amber's reaction as she said it; she had never had the chance to tell her about her own family. It was easier to talk about now than it had been then, when she'd tried and failed. "I spent most of my childhood in foster care, so it's always just been me."

Amber's face flickered with something undecipherable. A moment later, her hand found Drew's beneath the table, setting her skin on fire as their fingers locked together. Amber gave a gentle squeeze, and Drew eased slightly at the touch, the pad of her thumb brushing against warm skin. "You never told me that."

"I never got the chance." Her heart hammered painfully, and she kept waiting for the moment when Amber would pull away and she would be left without that touch again.

It never came.

"If you're free on Friday night, we're having a bit of an engagement party," Emily continued, wiping her hands on her napkin. She had barely touched her food, had cut it all up to make it look as though she had eaten more than she had. Drew knew, because she had done the same. "We'd love for you to come."

"Oh, I don't know —"

"Come," Amber interrupted with another squeeze of her hand. "I'd like you to come."

"Okay." Drew pressed her lips together and nodded in surrender. "Thank you."

She tried not to let the glimmer of hope reigniting in her stomach show as she forced a few more bites of chicken into her mouth, and then washed them down with an extra-large swig of brandy. It was just a party. They were just holding hands. It meant nothing.

It meant everything, though. Amber's hand in hers — it meant everything in the world.

∞ ∞ ∞

"My sister seems to really like you."

The voice behind Drew caused her to start, her wine swishing in its glass. They had run out of the brandy — John's doing, apparently. He was having an afternoon snooze in the spare bedroom now.

Kit held a tumbler of whiskey in his hand, ice clacking as he brought it to his lips and pretended to look interested in the Christmas tree. She had never seen one this large in an apartment before. It was a real, fresh-smelling pine that had shed its needles onto the carpet. Someone had bedazzled it from top to bottom with twinkling lights and tinsel — definitely not Amber, Drew thought.

A tree that meant family, love, warmth. It was the type of tree Drew had always dreamed of having as a child.

"Your sister doesn't like many people, so I'll take that as a compliment." Drew smirked. "Thank you."

"You took the words out of my mouth." Kit chuckled. "I've never seen her like this with anyone else. You're good for her."

The words caused Drew's cheeks to warm, and she glugged the rest of her wine while thinking of a way to respond. "I wouldn't go that far. We don't know each other all that well, really."

"I think when it's the right person, you know without really knowing." Kit frowned at his own words. "Did that make sense, or have I had one too many brandies?"

"No," Drew replied quietly, eyeing Amber intently. She stood by the sink with Emily, drying the clean plates and flinging them into the cupboard carelessly. Even now, with her back turned to her, Drew could feel the same familiarity, the same ease, she had always felt with her. Always would feel with her. Even if she was the only one of them who did. "No, it makes perfect sense."

Drew checked the clock on the wall and blanched. "I should be off, actually. We have another show tonight. Thank you, though, for having me. The dinner was lovely."

"No, it wasn't," Kit admitted dryly, placing both their glasses on the coffee table, "but you're very kind to lie."

"All right, then the company was lovely." She laughed and let him guide her into the hall.

Amber turned in the kitchen, drying her hands on the tea towel quickly. "You're leaving?"

"I have a show," Drew explained. "But I'll see you Friday?"

"Wait." Amber pushed past Kit and led Drew down to the door with a hand on her elbow. Drew wished she could hold that hand again. "Are you free tomorrow? I need to do some Christmas shopping and thought maybe you'd want to join."

Drew's heart lifted at the idea of another day with Amber. She was not used to this, not used to Amber being the one to initiate it all, to care. "I can meet you in the morning for a few hours or so."

"Great." The way Amber said it, breathy and relieved, was enough to set Drew grinning. "Then I'll see you tomorrow?"

"Tomorrow," Drew agreed. She didn't know whether to hug Amber or simply give a quick wave, so instead she did neither, shuffling out into the corridor instead. "Thank you for having me today."

"Thank you for coming," Amber replied softly, leaning against the door. "I'm glad you came, Drew. Really glad."

"I'm glad, too."

It was all Drew could articulate without embarrassing herself, so she left it at that. She would not frighten her away again. Not now.

The door did not click shut until Drew reached the end of the corridor, and even then she could feel Amber still close, still there.

Just as she always seemed to be. Just where she was supposed to be.

Twenty-Eight

"Tell me your name." The demand is no more than a soft sigh on Claude's lips — one he should not have made, and yet he can't help himself. It is no longer enough just to see the face of the thief bare of the black mask he'd been wearing a moment ago. He needs more of him. A thief in his own right — only it is not jewels he is after.

The thief's dark eyes narrow into black abysses that suck the dim light from the cloakroom. They suck Claude in, too. "You must think me a fool."

Claude scoffs, watching carefully as the thief picks up the pocket watch and prizes it open.

"Your watch is broken," he says.

"Is it?" Claude raises his eyebrows, though he is not particularly interested in the old watch.

The thief shakes his head in disbelief and pockets the watch. "You honestly mean to let me leave your ball with all of your most expensive possessions?"

Claude shrugs and motions to the door, which still hangs slightly ajar, in invitation. The delicate notes of the harp float through the crack, along with peals of laughter and conversation. He would bet all of the goods in the thief's pockets that not one of those *people are wondering where he is — he, their host. Wealth has still not bought him friends. It is why he does not care what the thief takes. Let him rob them all blind.*

The thief hesitates, glancing curiously to the door and back again. There is a tear in the seam by the shoulder of his jacket, made noticeable as he scratches his neck. "Why?"

Claude smirks at the question, pretending to browse the coats lined up on the racks as he contemplates his reply. "Because none of it means anything to me. Clearly, it means something to you."

"The jewels in my pocket, the ones you say mean nothing to you, could feed me for months," *he says harshly, features crinkling in disdain.*

"Would you rather me take them back?"

The thief steps away, covering his pockets protectively. It is all the answer Claude needs.

"That's what I thought."

Another glance to the door, and then back to Claude. A pause. "You are lonely."

Claude sneers at nothing in particular, though the question unearths him, uncovers him, leaves him feeling bare. "Everyone in that ballroom is lonely. Some are just better at hiding it."

The thief's dark eyes flicker with something unfathomable. They are so bottomless, so full. So familiar. "My name is Oliver."

"Oliver," *Claude repeats with a nod — and though he has gotten what he asked for, he feels no less satisfied. It is always his way; nothing will ever be enough for him — especially not where this stranger is involved. "Enjoy the rest of your night, Oliver."*

"You won't enjoy yours?"

Claude makes a show of pasting a wide grin to his face. "Of course I will."

Oliver tilts his head as though deciding something, and then says: "Come with me, then."

Claude swallows down a sputter. "Excuse me?"

"The city is beautiful in the snow, especially at night. Come see it with me."

"I can't," he replies, shaking his head slowly.

Oliver shrugs enough to rattle the coins in his pockets, and then puts his hand on the door. "Suit yourself."

He gathers his mask and slips out without a second glance, a flash of tulle and golden light spilling through the open door for only a moment. It is all the time that Claude needs to change his mind.

He puts his mask back on and flits out of the door after him.

∞ ∞ ∞

It took Amber half the morning to remember where she had seen that pocket watch before. In her dreams the last few nights, yes, but before that —

Drew. Drew had shown her that very pocket watch by the lake, had said all sorts of things that hadn't made any sense at the time.

Everything we were. Everything we've ever been. As though they had met before. As though she, too, had had these dreams.

But that would be impossible.

She tried to push it down when she met with Drew early the next morning. A hot chocolate was waiting for her too, and she swallowed it down as best she could as they window-shopped along the high street.

Amber was no longer in the mood to buy Christmas presents, not with thousands of unanswered questions surging through her.

When they came to an antiques shop, a dozen clock faces peering at them through their own reflections, Amber stopped and took a breath.

"The pocket watch."

Drew turned when she realized that Amber was no longer behind her, and paled slightly. "What?"

"The pocket watch that you showed me that day by the lake. Where did you get it?"

Drew looked anywhere but at her — a fact that only made Amber more anxious. "Amber, the things I said that day were stupid. It was all a big misunderstanding, and I've regretted it every day since."

Amber held a gloved hand up to silence her. Her breath was visible in front of her, the white clouds above them swollen with either snow or ice. The cold made everything clearer, sharper: Drew's face, less round now and more dimpled; her pale brown skin; her near black eyes, uptilted and lined with mascara. The same eyes that *he* had had in her dream. The thief. Oliver.

Every part of her was familiar. Had always been familiar.

And Drew had tried to tell her.

I see you everywhere I go, in everything I do, and I don't know why. She had said that at the tree house and blamed it on being drunk. Only she had not been drunk. She had just been waiting for Amber to feel it, too.

"Where did you get it?"

Drew frowned, the heels of her boots clicking as she took a step toward her. "I picked it up at the bazaar the day I met you."

"Why?"

"Why?" Drew repeated, gulping.

"Why did you buy it?"

"Amber, what is this about?"

"Why did you buy the watch, Drew?" Amber ground out impatiently.

Drew's lips opened and closed, tasting words that Amber could not hear. "Because," she breathed, "because it felt right. I don't know. It just... it found me."

Amber shook her head dazedly, shrinking into herself as a shopper almost collided with her. Perhaps she was just dreaming of the pocket watch because Drew had shown it to her once, and seeing her again had brought the memory of it back into her subconscious — but it didn't feel that way.

The dreams did not feel like dreams. They felt like memories.

Memories she had been hiding from until now.

"Why are you asking me this?"

"I don't know," Amber lied. And then: "Because I've been thinking about it a lot."

"Dreaming of it?" She lifted an eyebrow knowingly.

Amber nodded tersely.

Softening, Drew held out her hand. It felt to Amber like the only stable thing in the universe, now. "Come with me."

Come with me, then. The words the thief — Oliver — had uttered to Claude in that cloak-room. She saw him in Drew, in her inky-black hair and the beauty spots on her jaw. She saw Shay in her, too, though the image of him, red-haired and pale-skinned, was her opposite. And the pianist with the angel wings, the one Amber had remembered for the first time in the theater. Seeing him had been like unlocking a hoard of photographs she hadn't remembered existed, and she could not push them away or seal them shut again now.

She wanted to run from it. She wanted to run *to* it. She did the latter and took Drew's hand, if only in an attempt to understand, letting her pull her down the streets of Edinburgh.

Come with me, then.

Twenty-Nine

Drew hadn't dared let go of Amber's hand as she'd led her to the museum for fear of her running away. All this time, she had waited. All this time, she had stood in this very spot alone — the only one who remembered.

That had changed today. Without having to ask, Drew knew that Amber remembered: she could recognize her fear and bewilderment for what it was, because she had felt it not that long ago, too, and had been coming to terms with it ever since.

Drew knew Amber, though; she knew she would not accept it so easily. She had to be careful.

The oil painting was as familiar to Drew as her own reflection. A silhouette of two men running down an old street lined with gas lamps and flecked with snow. A thick white blanket glistened beneath their feet, the sky tinged purple with the coming dawn. Drew had no idea who had painted it, had not recognized the French name nor been able to draw any links with research. It might have depicted any couple, except that the inscription beneath read *Paris, 1817*. They were close enough to Drew's own memories that she had known, had stared at it for hours upon hours since moving here. When Amber had been gone, this was all that had remained to remind her.

She risked a glance at Amber and found tears in her eyes. Drew wished she could kiss them away, but knew better than to try. She needed time. Space, perhaps. Perhaps this meant nothing to her at all. None of it had ever made sense. It wouldn't start now, with just a painting that could easily be passed off as a coincidence.

"How...?" Amber breathed.

"I don't know," Drew replied gently. "I came here a few weeks after moving and just... found it here. It reminded me of you."

"It doesn't make sense," she said, and Drew knew she was no longer talking about the painting.

"I know. It never did."

Amber tore her eyes from the painting, her silvery gaze piercing through Drew like the point of a blade. Drew's entire body prickled with the impact. "What did you do with the pocket watch?"

"I threw it into the sea after..." Drew couldn't say it. She didn't want to think about that day, had tried to block it out of her memory a hundred times. But like every other image, dream, feeling that Drew had of Amber and their lives together, it would not be chased away so easily.

Amber seemed to understand, nodding numbly. "Why now? Why is this happening to me now, when you...?"

"Mabel said that it might take longer for you, or that you might never remember," Drew said. "Perhaps you weren't ready to believe it until now."

"Mabel," she repeated, wonder clear in her expression. And then: "You remembered because of the pocket watch?"

"Yes, but not just because of it. I saw you and a part of me just... knew." Drew worried at her lip, trying to make sense of it herself. "Maybe throwing the watch away, destroying it, broke something. We never usually met more than once in our lifetimes."

"Always the thirtieth of October," Amber recalled. Drew was impressed: it had taken her far longer to realize that the dates had been consistent.

"Like I said, I think I broke something. Maybe put an end to this for good." The thought made Drew's chest ache. This had been painful in every lifetime, yes, but better to have met Amber and lost her knowing they would meet again than to face the future without her in it at all. Even just in the past few days, she had shown Drew what a home felt like. She had taught her to love and to dare. She had gotten her here, living a life she was proud of, pursuing the thing she loved most: the piano. Who would Drew be without her in the next lifetime? The one after? "I think... I think perhaps that this time it really was just a coincidence that we met. It doesn't follow the pattern at all."

"Excuse me." Amber's voice wavered as she darted away from the painting, and away from Drew.

Straight out of the museum.

Thirty

It was snowing.

It was snowing, and all that Amber could see were horses pulling coaches along through gray sludge in the cobblestone streets of Paris. She could see herself, Claude, lifting her arms to the sky and tasting the cold flakes on her tongue as Oliver laughed. She could see snow angels and feel her teeth chattering as she led Oliver to shelter. She could see it all. She could remember everything.

Drew stumbled out of the museum behind her, surprise evident on her features. White flakes already dusted her dark hair, her shoulders, her tartan scarf. It hadn't stuck on the pavement yet, still dissolving where it landed.

"Amber." She mouthed her name like a prayer, the Christmas lights of the shop window behind her haloing her figure in gold.

A car horn brought Amber back, and she realized that she had been standing in the road. She stepped back onto the curb, narrowly avoiding an umbrella passing by. The shoppers on the high street were practically dripping with cheer, linking arms and sipping from Starbucks cups. Oblivious.

Too much. It was too much.

Fate did not exist. Fate was not real. Past lives were not something that should be remembered. And yet Drew stood as proof in front of her, patiently waiting in the middle of passing hoards of people for Amber to say something... anything.

Amber gulped and wiped her damp hair from her eyes, teeth chattering. "What now? What's supposed to happen now? Shall I tell you that I'll see you again in another century or so, leave it at that? Shall I run into your arms and declare you my soul mate?" Panic thickened her voice, brought a lump to her throat. "What now, Drew?"

"I'm not sure we have another century, Amber," she said quietly, pulling her out of the way of the crowds. Amber tore her arm out of her grip as though Drew's touch burned. "It's never happened like this before. It might never happen like this again."

"So this is our last chance?"

Drew shrugged as though it were simple. "Maybe."

"And you're okay with this?"

Drew's face was damp from the snow, hair starting to glisten with it as she nestled into her scarf. The city's lights reflected in her eyes as she blinked. "I've had a lot longer to come to terms with this than you. I've realized that I can't make you be with me, make you feel things, see things the way that I do. I've realized it might not ever be the right time for us." Her voice lowered when she murmured, "But I want it to be. I wish it could be. I have been tethered to you since the moment I met you, and that hasn't gone away. I can't tell you what happens next, Amber. I can't help you understand it, because I don't, either. All I can say is that when you're ready — *if* you're ready — I'm here... and I still dream of you."

The words were kindling for the ever-smoldering fire within Amber. How she burned for her — had always burned for her. How the remaining embers from that fire did not crackle up into the sky, but into her veins, where they prickled and seared through every inch of her. How they thawed her frozen bones, just for a moment.

Just as Amber softened, taking a step toward her, Drew checked her phone and glanced at her apologetically. "I have rehearsal soon. I'm so sorry. I want to talk about this, though."

"You should go," Amber agreed, jaw clenching. "I'll come and find you before the show."

"I'll be backstage." Drew's lips pursed into a thin line, as though she didn't trust Amber's words. As though she might not see her again after this. Amber, though, didn't shy away when Drew gripped her hand and squeezed. "Wait for me. Please."

The damp seeped into Amber's gloves and made everything feel wrong, cold. The hot chocolate, too, tasted bitter on her tongue. This felt like another goodbye. The last goodbye, perhaps.

But Amber let her go, anyway. Let her disappear into the crowd.

Thirty-One

"I have to go."

Claude is sodden down to the bone, his hands and feet made of ice, and yet he turns even colder at the words. Beside him, Oliver has made no move to sit up. His hair is still damp, curling at the nape of his neck.

The fire is their only respite. It hisses and sparks across the logs until they are burnt to cinders in the fireplace, casting guttering shadows across their faces. They have been this way all night. Claude wishes they could be this way forever.

"Stay a little longer," he pleads, fingers dancing across Oliver's scalp before knotting themselves in his hair. Oliver melts into his touch for only a moment before tugging Claude's hand down across his shoulder and playing with the silver band on his ring finger — as though pointing to all the reasons he cannot give in to Claude's wishes. The ring has lived there for only a few months. He is still not used to it, even now. It was an arranged thing he had no say in. Not like Oliver. Not like this, now.

"Your guests will have realized by now that their possessions are missing."

"You overestimate them." It is true, though:

dawn has broken across Paris, the pale orange light bleeding through the lace curtains of Claude's bedroom. By now his guests will have sobered, will probably be waking to find that the jewelry they wore and the coins they bore were no longer where they left them last night.

Oliver finally pulls away, tugging on his socks and shoes and buttoning his white shirt back up. "I can't risk it. I have to go."

Claude stands, shrugging the fleece blanket off his shoulders and raking a hand through his unkempt hair. His bones still ache with cold.

He could plead again. He could tell him that Oliver is safe here, with him. He does not dare let his pride falter any more than it already has, though. He will not stoop to that, not even now. Sooner or later, he would still have to say goodbye anyway.

Instead, he lets Oliver kiss him on the forehead, and then the lips, just once.

Oliver pulls something from his jacket: the pocket watch, with the chain dangling from his palm. He slips it into Claude's breast pocket gently, fingers lingering by his open shirt for just a moment. Claude's skin tightens.

"You don't want to keep it?"

"I think I've taken enough," Oliver whispers. And then he is at the door, both too far away and closer than he will ever be again. He rests his hat on his head, tipping it to Claude with a sad, knowing smile painted on his lips. "Until we meet again, Claude Augustin."

"Goodbye, Oliver," Claude murmurs, and then turns his back to him. He does not want to watch him leave, knowing that this time, he cannot follow.

The door clicks shut unbearably slowly, and then time stops altogether.

∞∞∞

Amber had searched the theater high and low for Drew and found her touching up her lipstick in the bathroom alone. She was beautiful even under the fluorescents, all dewy skin, with her hair straightened behind her shoulders. It only made what she was about to do harder.

How easily she could forget it and fall into her if she chose to. But that was not Amber. And this would never be a happy ending, not with them. There was plenty of proof to show her that. Centuries' worth.

"Amber." Drew's voice shook as she caught Amber's eye in the reflection, clicking the lid on her lipstick and sliding it into her pocket quickly. "I didn't think you'd come."

Amber took a deep, wavering breath, clutching her backpack just for something to hold. She did not dare look in the mirror, did not dare face who stood there. She did not want to see this version of them — of her.

"I came to say goodbye."

Drew faltered back as though the words

were a physical blow, her face crinkling with pain. It caused bile to rise in Amber's throat. She hated herself for it.

"I'm going home early," she said. "Going to catch a late train. I need some time alone to think."

"You don't have to do that," Drew croaked hoarsely. "If space is what you need, I'll give it to you. You should spend time with your family."

Amber shook her head, clenching her jaw in determination. She wouldn't change her mind now. "I need space from everyone. Everything. I can't get that here."

"And there's nothing that I can say to stop you?"

"We've done that before," Amber replied. "More than enough times. I think it's time we said goodbye and meant it."

"Why?" Drew's voice cracked with tears. She gripped Amber's hands tightly. "Why can't it be different this time? We've already found one another without the watch, without any of it. This could be the right time. This could be what we've been waiting for."

"No." Amber's tone was flat, hollow, and she despised herself for it as she pulled away from Drew's grip.

"No?" Drew frowned.

"No," she repeated. "I won't pretend as though I believe in any of this. I can't be somebody's soul mate, or whatever it is you think we are. I'm not that person."

"I never said you were. I never asked that of you," Drew said. "I never asked you to be anyone but yourself, as you are now."

"Well, this is myself," she retorted, hands slapping at her sides in frustration. "I run away from things I don't understand. I go where I'm comfortable, safe. I won't force myself into a relationship because I've been hallucinating, or because of a few paintings, or because apparently we met a few times in other lives. Do you realize how stupid it sounds? How ridiculous it would be to believe it? And even if we did, all it seems to have caused is pain."

"If you think that, why are you here?" Drew snapped, eyes ablaze. "Why not just go? You're right; we have done this before. Couldn't you have just said goodbye and left it at that — or did you *want* to hurt me tonight?"

Amber chewed on her lip, heart shredding itself into ribbons. God, she hated herself, hated hurting Drew again. Did she even believe the things she was saying? Or was she just a coward? The same coward who had left Sidney in 1917, who had watched Oliver go in 1817, and Shay in 1717. But if that was their fate — to leave, to be left — why drag it out now only to lose her later?

"No," she answered finally, defeat seeping into her voice. Her stomach twisted with regret, and yet she could not keep doing this. She couldn't keep losing her. It would be better for them both to break the cycle. "I'm sorry. I shouldn't have come.

Goodbye, Drew."

Drew did not say it back. She didn't look at her at all, instead gripping the edge of the sink and staring into the drain.

It should have made it easier to leave, but it didn't. None of this had ever been easy.

No matter how many times history repeated itself, Amber could not get used to losing Drew.

Thirty-Two

Shay riding away beside his brother, the forest burying his retreating figure with its dying leaves while Aishling can only watch; the sound of Oliver's retreating footsteps down marbled hallways, while Claude can only listen; Grace slamming the door shut on Sidney, while her stomach pleads with her to turn back. This was what Amber remembered as she waited on the cold train platform. In all of them, her heart had wrenched and her body hadn't wanted to let go. It still didn't.

Yet she had done it again. She had walked away again — to prevent the pain she would feel later on, when it inevitably ended, as it always had before.

The station was an endless, empty tunnel, every sound echoing off the walls as trains whined their departure. A seed of anxiety had planted itself in Amber's stomach the moment she had gotten here, making everything feel wrong, as though she were not herself anymore. As though she were in the wrong place at the wrong time, watching herself as though from the eyes of someone else.

She glanced around, knees shaking. The cold seeped from the bench and through her jeans, writhing in her until it found her twisting stomach.

A woman sat on the platform opposite, hard-faced and wrinkled. Alone.

Behind Amber, a man who had grinned toothlessly at her as she sat paced from one edge of the platform to the other, wafting the smell of his dusty, stale clothes. Alone.

Amber sat alone, too. But she didn't have to, not if she chose. Drew was probably playing the piano, still, her music singing out to a captivated audience. Twice now had Amber left her in this life.

Twice now had she regretted it.

She stood up just as the train rolled in, watching in a trance as it came to a stop. The door landed directly in front of her, teasing her. But the yellow lights of the train were not appealing to her, nor was the cold whoosh of air it brought in with it. Amber's pulse throbbed in her ears. Could she do this again? Could she walk away from this again?

But she couldn't be somebody's soul mate. She couldn't rely on the universe or a damn watch that was now lost at sea to give her the life she wanted, or to keep her safe from any more loss. Better to be alone. Better to not —

"Leaving without saying goodbye?"

She turned to find Kit standing at the end of the platform, hands in his pockets and lips downturned in disappointment. His hair hung into his eyes limply, cheeks flushed with the cold — and perhaps from racing to get here in time.

Amber had sent him a simple text telling him that she was going home early and that she would see him and Emily in the new year. Clearly it hadn't warded him off as she had hoped.

"What are you doing here?"

"What are *you* doing here?" he retorted, glaring. "I thought we were past this."

"This isn't about you," she said, stepping away from the train so that she could hear him over the rattling engine.

"Then what is it about?" Anger danced in his eyes. "Drew?"

Amber shook her head, unable to answer, unable to look at him at all. The faint lights above were making her tired… and she was cold, so cold, and still felt so wrong.

"Does Dad know you're here?"

"No," he answered, "and he won't have to if you come home now."

"It's complicated."

"It's not complicated," Kit returned calmly. "You're doing what you always do. Pushing people away. Running away from what you really feel."

She scowled. "You don't know anything."

"I know enough. You did it to me plenty of times."

"Is that why you came here?" she questioned. "To get in one last dig before I go?"

"I came to take you home, you idiot." He sighed hopelessly through gritted teeth. "Do you like Drew?"

"It doesn't —"

Kit interrupted, holding out his hand to silence her. "Do. You. Like. Drew?"

Amber closed her eyes and nodded. *Like* was a diluted word for what Amber felt for Drew. Drew overwhelmed her, made her *feel*. "Yes."

"Do you trust her?"

Did she? She had never given Drew the chance to prove anything. They had never even had time to explore that part of themselves, not in any version of themselves. When she was with her, she felt safe, yes, but she also felt as though she were leaning over the edge of a precipice, as though if she took the final step, Amber would fall to something unknown — especially now, without the watch and without their usual pattern. Perhaps the chance that things could be different this time only made that more terrifying. At least before she had always known it would end, could prepare herself for it.

"I don't know," Amber admitted. "Maybe."

"Okay," he said. "Isn't it worth a try, even if you're afraid?"

"I'm not afraid," she lied.

"Ma'am?"

Amber whirled around. The conductor stood behind her, a whistle suspended in her hands impatiently. "Are you getting on this train?"

"I..."

She didn't have the answer. Helplessly, she

looked back to Kit. His face had softened, his eyebrows raised as though he, too, wanted to know the answer. Behind him, an old-fashioned clock was suspended above the station.

Ten thirty. Of course.

Drew would be finishing her show now, probably. Perhaps she would be going home to an empty apartment. Could Amber live with never seeing her again, while always having that tug in her chest? Always having the memories of her, of them, of all of it?

But if she tried, only for it to end badly —

Amber couldn't think about that.

"I can't force you to stay," Kit said. "I can't force you to do anything, but I think you like Drew, and I think that scares you because you've been holding everybody at arm's length since Mum died. It's okay to be scared, Amber. Just don't let it ruin something good. Mum wouldn't want that for you. You know that."

The seconds ticked by, and with them, the regret. Amber thought of everything she had felt, every heartbeat that had belonged to Drew in this life and in the others that had come before. She could keep pretending she didn't want this, keep saying that she didn't understand, but she did: Drew was hers. Drew would always be hers. And she had left her broken, again.

She had let her go so many times before because of things she could not control. This time, she had made a choice — and she knew now, with that awful, sharp rock in her throat and the way her whole world felt crumpled and wrong, that she had made the wrong one. Drew made her happy. Even without all of the things that came with her — the past, the memories — Drew would still have made her happy. It wasn't just about who they were anymore. It was about what they could be if Amber only gave it a chance.

If she could only push her pride and fears aside, stop letting fate decide for her. They might never get this chance again. *It might never happen like this again.*

"No," she said to the conductor finally over her shoulder, stepping away from the train. There was no uncertainty in her voice. She knew. Had always known. Every breath, every step for at least three hundred years had led her here. She had been a fool to fight it, to not recognize it sooner. "No, I'm not getting on the train."

The conductor shook her head in exasperation and blew the whistle, waving the driver away. It was gone. Her way out was gone. And she was relieved not to be on it.

Kit blew out a breath of relief. "You're an idiot, you know that?"

"I know," Amber agreed quietly, running a hand over her face. The coldness of her own fingers awakened her, let her know what she had to do next. She had to follow the pull. She looked steadily up at her brother, heart hammering against her chest, and said: "I'm sorry to be such a pain in the arse, but I need you to take me to the theater."

Kit grinned as though he had been waiting to hear the words all along.

Thirty-Three

The streets were empty, the night a thick blanket that was neither warm nor soothing for Drew. She had given anything that was left of her to the audience tonight, and now she felt hollow, her fingers raw — her heart, too.

She had debated going after Amber, had debated chasing her to the train station and begging her to stay, but she couldn't face another rejection or another goodbye, another memory to put in the bank and cash in on in one hundred years' time, when the next version of her lived through another heartache. If they even got that chance, now that the pattern had changed.

So she walked down the back street with slow steps, each click of her heels bringing with it another aching pang to her chest. She wished she had never remembered any of it at all.

"Drew."

The voice was nothing more than a feeble breath behind her, so much so that she might have passed it off for wishful thinking or a gust of wind — until she turned and found Amber behind her, hands free of any luggage. Tears glittered in her eyes, her lips pressed into a trembling, timid line.

Drew half wondered if she was hallucinating as the cold wind tore through them, and tightened her arms around herself to keep her heart from falling out of her chest entirely. "Amber," she whispered hoarsely. "I thought you left."

"I couldn't," Amber said. "I couldn't leave you because I don't want to."

Drew swallowed her tears, unable to utter a word.

"I realized that I can't wait for you again." Amber inched closer, shivering against the cold. "I want you now. I want you always. I won't wait any longer for the chance to find out why we've always been pulled together. I want to find out now, while we still can. No more walking away, no more hiding."

"But you don't believe in any of it," Drew pointed out, unable to hide her disbelief. "You didn't want this."

"I was afraid to want this. I meant what I said: I don't know if I can be your soul mate. But I can be *something* for you. I can at least give us a chance."

"I meant what I said, too," Drew breathed. "I don't want you to be anything but yourself. I don't expect anything from you. I don't care about what's happened in the past, Amber. I only care about who we are now."

Amber tangled her fingers into Drew's hair, and Drew's lids fluttered shut in response, tears slipping down her cheeks.

"I still don't understand any of it," Amber said. "But maybe we don't have to. Maybe it's okay that we just *know*."

"I've known," Drew murmured. "I've known since the moment I met you. I belong with you, Amber Hall. Always have, always will."

"Good." Her lips spread into a soft smile — perhaps the most beautiful thing that Drew had ever seen. "Because I never want to say goodbye to you again."

"Then don't," Drew begged. "Don't."

She let out a feeble sob that was stolen from her as Amber's lips pressed against hers. They fell away from the shadows of the street, and away from the world entirely. It was only them, and everything they had been, and everything they could be: tethered, always.

Drew let her lips graze Amber's birthmark around her eye, down her cheek. She had dreamed of that birthmark so many times — dreamed of *her* so many times. Her Amber. Her gold. Here, giving herself to Drew completely.

Finally, their story was not a sad one. Finally, it was beginning rather than ending.

Something clicked into place that Drew had never felt before — not in this life, nor in any other. They were not Aishling and Shay, Claude and Oliver, Sidney and Grace.

They were Amber and Drew. They would make their own rules, now, decide their own fates.

No more waiting. No more goodbyes.

Epilogue

Kit's apartment brimmed with people Amber didn't know — people she had had to make small talk with all evening. It was her idea of hell, but she did it for her brother. Her brother, who was stumbling through the kitchen to her now.

"Hey, stranger." He squeezed her shoulders lightly, eyes creasing with a smile. She had never seen him so happy, so bright.

"Enjoying your party?" Amber raised an eyebrow, bringing her champagne flute to her mouth and sipping lightly. It was an effort to swallow down the bubbly, sweet drink. She would much rather have had a cup of tea.

Kit nodded, eyes falling to Emily. She stood in the hallway, talking to a woman she'd introduced earlier as her best friend. Her grin was unshakeable, too, her green eyes glittering. Once, Amber would not have even noticed that happiness, would not have cared. Now she wanted to be a part of it all — and she wanted it for herself, too. With Drew.

"I'm glad you decided to stay, Amber," he said. "Really glad."

Amber allowed herself to soften only

slightly. "I wouldn't miss it. I'm happy for you, Kit. Really."

"Thank you." He pulled her into an awkward side hug, ruffling up her hair the way he had done when they were children. "I'm happy for you, too. You deserve something good, even if you are a fool for almost running from it."

Amber rolled her eyes at such soppy words and shoved his chest lightly. Still, her gaze flitted instinctively to the Christmas tree, where Drew was having a conversation with her father, offering a polite nod here and there, as though her body had already known where Drew would be — as though she no longer had to look for her, and would not ever have to again.

As though sensing Amber's attention, her dark eyes lifted suddenly, and they locked on one another across the room. She looked beautiful tonight in the soft, silvery Christmas lights, her hair cascading in waves around her and her lips painted red. Amber still could not believe she was hers.

It terrified her sometimes still, but she did not regret staying. Kit was right: she deserved to be happy. Perhaps they were indeed soul mates, or perhaps the universe was indifferent to whether they were pulled together or not, but either way, Amber did not care. She had hidden away from love for too long. It was time to start letting people in again.

"Thanks for making me see sense," she replied finally, cheeks flushing as Drew's gaze fell away and Amber returned to her place in the kitchen. "It's been a long time coming." Centuries, perhaps.

"Well, some things are worth waiting for," said Kit with a nudge. "Just don't run off again, eh?"

"I won't," Amber promised, slipping an hors d'oeuvre into her mouth and then spitting it straight back out into a tissue with a dramatic heave. Her face crumpled in disgust, the taste of something sour and foul lingering on her tongue. "Jesus, what is this?"

"Hmm?" Kit had drifted off beside her, glassy-eyed and watching Emily's every move intently. And then she was waving him over, and Amber knew she had lost him for good. "Oh, just some goat-cheese parcel thing. I don't know."

"The city changed you!" she called to Kit's back as he shuffled past her to get to Emily, throwing the tissue away and gulping down the awful aftertaste with another swig of champagne. It did not help one bit.

Her focus returned to the Christmas tree. Drew stood alone now, admiring the decorations with her back to Amber. As though being pulled by a fishing line, Amber set off toward her without thought, searching through her pocket for the familiar small box she had been hiding all night. It was still there, safe and sound.

"Guess who?" Amber cupped her hands

over Drew's eyes as she reached her.

"Someone with terrible breath," Drew replied with a smirk. "Have you been eating those fancy cheese thingies in the kitchen?"

Amber tutted in offense and dropped her hands. "Well, I was going to give you an early Christmas present, but now I don't think I will."

Amber pulled out the box. It was wrapped terribly, the bow all wonky and random strips of tape sticking out everywhere. Perhaps she should have asked Emily to do it. Her presents already sat in neat little boxes beneath the tree.

Drew didn't seem to mind, her eyes widening in soft appreciation. "You didn't have to get me anything."

"I wanted to," Amber insisted, pressing the gift into Drew's hands. She took it with a scolding glance, tearing into the foil paper with hands that shook ever so slightly. Amber's own heart was hammering. Was it too soon for presents? Perhaps it was a stupid idea. Perhaps she should snatch it back now before Drew opened —

Too late. Drew let the paper fall to the floor as her fingers grazed over the black box with a frown.

"It's stupid, really." Amber shook her head nervously, biting down on her bottom lip.

Carefully, Drew pulled the lid off the box to reveal what was inside: a small round golden locket. Her breath caught as she pulled it out and held it to the light, cheeks flushed.

"Open it," Amber urged.

Drew did, unclasping the gilded case. Inside, a small clockface ticked. The time was ten thirty — but no longer frozen there.

"Amber…" she breathed.

"A new watch for a new life," Amber said. "Together, if you'd like."

Drew's eyes fluttered shut for a moment. When she opened, they were filled with tears. "Thank you. I love it."

Amber only nodded bashfully, taking the necklace from her and fastening it around Drew's neck on her tiptoes. Tonight she wore a shimmering slip dress that dipped down her back. Amber used it to her advantage, letting her fingers brush against the bare nape of Drew's neck, the knots at the top of her spine, down to her shoulder blades. She watched goosebumps rise in response to her touch, and Drew shivered in disappointment when Amber finally pulled away.

Later. They had all of the time in the world to explore one another now. The thought caused goosebumps to prickle on Amber's own skin.

"I feel bad," Drew whispered. "I only brought two pieces of thread."

She opened up her own hand to reveal two strands of red running like a river across the lines of Drew's palms. Amber shook her head and held out her hand, letting Drew tie one around her finger before returning the favor. And then, as Drew had done the first time, Amber kissed her knuckle as though to seal the knot.

"I can't believe you remember that."

"I remember everything," said Drew, and Amber knew exactly what she meant.

Amber rested her head on Drew's shoulder and turned her attention to the Christmas tree. The spice of Drew's perfume curled around her like a second pair of arms — so familiar, so warm, so *Drew*. They were the only people who existed, their surroundings dulling to a low hum that could not touch them.

"Your father and I had an interesting conversation," Drew murmured against Amber's hair.

Amber laughed. "I saw him collar you earlier. What did he say?"

"He told me that he was planning on staying here over Christmas instead of going home."

Amber lifted her head up to look at her, narrowing her eyes. "Did he now?"

Drew nodded, the corner of her mouth rising amusedly. "He did."

Amber feigned a dramatic huff and put her head back on Drew's shoulder. This time Drew's arm snaked around her waist. The muffled ticking of the locket synchronized with her own heartbeat. "I guess it's decided, then. Nobody told me."

"He also said that it was your idea." Amber could hear the laughter bubbling in her voice as her grip tightened.

"Fine. I might have suggested it, yes."

Drew planted a soft kiss in her hair. "Don't

worry, I won't tell anyone you've gone soft."

"Don't," she warned. "I'll never hear the end of it from my brother."

Drew vibrated with a chuckle. Amber silenced her with a kiss. How far they had strayed from the past versions of themselves, destined always to lose one another. Amber had vowed never to lose Drew again. She wanted this: here, now. There would be no more "until we meet again."

For the very first time, they were both exactly where they were supposed to be: together. Amber could imagine all of the past versions of themselves — Aishling and Shay, Claude and Oliver, Grace and Sidney — closing their eyes and sighing with relief. They had gotten here at long last. They could rest knowing that, now.

The new watch ticked contentedly between their hearts as they melted into one another again.

It would not stop — not for a long, long time.

Books By This Author

A Haunting At Hartwell Hall

Safe And Sound

Handmade With Love

Partners In Crime

Holding On To Bluebell Lodge

No Love Lost

Paint Me Yours

Along For The Ride

Printed in Great Britain
by Amazon